# Allison remembered the kiss

There was no denying the attraction, at least on her part. She had found their pretend kiss—her idea to show the townspeople that Dell was a desirable man—very, very exciting. And unfulfilling. Her body clamored for more. Her heart knew better than to entertain the idea.

Dell turned onto the private road that led to the ranch. He slowed down after he'd rounded the first turn, stopped the car and turned to Allison.

"Come here," was all he said in an expressionless voice.

Allison gulped. "Why?"

"Just do it," he said, mimicking her words in the diner when she'd told him to kiss her in front of Lucille.

She inched closer to him, and he put his hands on her upper arms and lifted her onto his lap. Then he kissed her, but this time there was no hesitation in the motion. His lips were warm and demanding, and when he urged her lips apart Allison didn't think to protest the intimacy. He made love to her mouth for long, body-melting moments, until Allison whimpered with need and desire. He released her then.

"What was that for?" she asked, embarrassed to hear the way her voice shook.

"I don't like being played for a fool."

**Kristine Rolofson** is one busy and amazing lady. The author of over twenty books, all published by Harlequin, she is also a mother of six! A Rhode Island native, she now resides in the same town where she spent her childhood. Writing about family life is one of the strong themes in her books. *Romantic Times* gave her last book, *The Texan Takes a Wife*, a 4¹/₂ Gold Star (their very highest rating) and had this to say: "Jam-packed with vividly appealing characters, this romantic romp captivates our hearts and delivers extraordinary reading bliss."

Kristine's story *A Touch of Texas* will be part of the Hometown Reunion series in March. She will also have a Love & Laughter book available in the fall of 1997.

The next Boots & Booties book is *The Next Man in Texas* (on sale in March).

## Books by Kristine Rolofson

HARLEQUIN TEMPTATION

507—PLAIN JANE'S MAN
548—JESSIE'S LAWMAN
560—MAKE-BELIEVE HONEYMOON
569—THE COWBOY
604—THE TEXAN TAKES A WIFE
617—THE LAST MAN IN MONTANA  Boots & Booties 1

# Kristine Rolofson
# THE ONLY MAN IN WYOMING

## *Harlequin Books*

TORONTO • NEW YORK • LONDON
AMSTERDAM • PARIS • SYDNEY • HAMBURG
STOCKHOLM • ATHENS • TOKYO • MILAN
MADRID • WARSAW • BUDAPEST • AUCKLAND

With love to my very wonderful mother-in-law,
Virginia Rolofson

ISBN 0-373-25721-X

THE ONLY MAN IN WYOMING

RIVER OF NO RETURN. Lost River Valley. The signs, few and far between on the isolated road, were just a little too symbolic of Allison Reynolds' predicament. Now she'd made yet another wrong turn and found herself on a gravel road, somewhere in Wyoming, with no idea where to go next. She studied the road map while the babies, tucked in identical car seats, began to fuss. She could go straight and hope to run into a town eventually.

Unless, of course, she was heading west by mistake, in which case she would bump into a mountain range and never be heard from again.

Sylvie, never patient, began to cry. And Sophie, willing to go along with her twin's complaints, added her own pitiful sobs to the noise inside the car. Allison closed her eyes and prayed for patience. And quiet. And for a four-star hotel to appear in front of the Ford Probe, which had been making a terrible racket since Allison had guided it across a pothole the size of a moon crater a few miles back.

All in all, it was not a good day. It was not an especially good month or even a good year, Allison decided. She opened her eyes and turned around to comfort the children.

"Sweethearts," she crooned, hoping her voice sounded calmer than she felt. "It's okay. We're going to be out of this nasty car soon." They looked at her with tear-filled blue eyes and continued to scream. "Auntie Allison will fix everything and we'll be on our way."

Auntie Allison wanted to run screaming back to Kansas City. She got out of the car and checked the tires on the driver's side of the little white hatchback. It wasn't exactly a family car, but she'd had it for six years and it had served her well. White and sporty, with a small back seat, it had held up for four years and seventy-three thousand miles. Until they'd crossed into Wyoming, that is. Allison avoided stepping in the muddier ruts in the road and walked around to the other side. The front left wheel looked a little crooked, as if it was about to fall right off its axle. Allison's heart sank.

What had ever made her think she could do this alone?

DELL JONES hated to go to town, especially near the end of calving season, but there'd been no choice. He'd had to go to the bank, get the week's mail and pick up the supplies for Calvin. Running out of coffee when all of them were working half the night constituted a real emergency as far as Dell was concerned. He shoved the pickup into low gear and rounded the crest of the hill, and that's when he saw her. Her golden hair hung in fluffy waves past her shoulders and the body encased in jeans and a bright blue sweater was everything delicate and fragile. Dell didn't recognize her, and he figured he knew everyone in the county.

He wondered for a brief moment if she were real, and he took his foot off the gas pedal and watched her walk around the front of the car and kneel on the driver seat. That long hair hung down to a particularly shapely rear, and Dell gulped. She was real, all right, and she was in trouble. There was no other reason for a woman to be parked on the side of this road, not at the end of April. It was too early for tourists and too late for hunters.

Dell parked the truck in the middle of the road, kept the engine running, and rolled down his window. He didn't want to scare her. Women were jumpy these days, and he didn't blame them. Damn, he wished he'd shaved. Not that it would do any good. An ugly mug was an ugly mug, with or without whiskers.

She'd turned around and looked at him. Blue eyes. Oh, Lord, of course she'd have blue eyes and look like an angel, heart-shaped face and all.

"Ma'am? Can I help you?"

The woman looked uncertain, and didn't move, so Dell tried again. "I live near here," he said. "On the Lazy J ranch. Do you need help?"

The angel nodded, then sighed. "I'm lost and I think my car is damaged. I was just going to call a gas station and see if I could get towed to town. Then I realized I didn't know what town I'm close to."

"You're thirty miles from the nearest town, ma'am, and Wells City is a real small town at that. You want me to take a look at your car?"

She studied him with a pair of big blue eyes, then said, "Please" with a touch of reluctance, so Dell moved his truck out of the middle of the road and shut off the ignition. He thought he heard babies crying, and as he approached the car he tipped his hat from his forehead and peered through the car windows. Sure enough, two little babies were screaming at the top of their lungs.

"Lady," he drawled, turning to look down at her. "What in hell are you doing out here?"

"I'm lost," she confessed. "And I hit a pothole and now the right front wheel is crooked."

"Where were you going?"

"Seattle."

He turned and stared at her. He'd expected her to say "Cheyenne" or "Salt Lake," not a city that was still hundreds of miles and a couple of states away. She followed him around to the other side of the car, where Dell hunkered down and examined the wheel.

"Can I drive on it?" she asked.

He shook his head. "I'm guessing you have a cracked or broken axle. When that goes, it'll make a flat tire seem like a picnic in comparison." Raindrops started falling, and the sky darkened into a charcoal gray. It would be dark soon, and though the Lazy J was in no shape for guests, and no matter how much he wanted to get home, there was no way Dell could leave the woman here with her car phone and her hopes for a tow truck.

"Did you say the nearest town is thirty miles away?"

"Yes, ma'am, but I'd be glad to take you to my ranch. It's five miles, as the crow flies, from here."

"Thank you," she said, very politely. She backed up a step. "I can't. The babies—"

"Are hungry," he finished for her. "I can take you into town in the morning. You're welcome to stay at the ranch tonight and I'll have one of my men tow your car to town tomorrow."

"I couldn't possibly. I mean," she said, her cheeks flushing. "I mean, it's very nice of you, but—"

"You don't know me." He didn't smile, but he wanted to. "Tell you what," he said, pulling his battered wallet from his back pocket and handing it to her. "Give the county sheriff's office a call and see what they say about Wendell Jones."

She took the wallet and opened it, glanced at his picture and back at him. "You must think I'm being pretty paranoid."

"Nope. You're being smart. There should be a card in there listing telephone numbers."

"Thank you."

He waited by her car while she made the call. The babies had stopped screaming, though they sighed and hiccuped as if they had given up trying to make themselves understood. They looked at Dell and their bottom lips quivered. Twins, of course. The back of the car was packed with duffel bags, boxes of disposable diapers and a small cooler. There were pink blankets and bright rubber toys crammed between the car seats, plastic pacifiers everywhere. The babies stared at him, and Dell smiled. He waggled his fingers and wondered if they liked cowboys waving at them. They didn't seem to mind.

He heard the woman's quiet voice on the phone and knew it was only a matter of a few minutes more before he would be bundling all her belongings into his truck and heading home before the rain started in earnest.

It was supposed to be a hell of a night, with another storm coming. Already the wind was blowing colder air, the kind that got in a man's bones and wouldn't let go. Dell shivered and one of the babies smiled.

"All set," the woman said, stepping out of the car to move toward him. "They were very nice."

"And?"

She smiled, and he noticed there was a tiny dimple

in her left cheek. "Someone named Officer Baker told me I should thank my lucky stars that you came along. He said there was a storm coming, so go home with you and worry about finding a mechanic tomorrow."

Dell nodded. "Good advice. You going to take it before we both get wet?"

She stuck out her hand. "Yes, Mr. Jones. I'm Allison Reynolds."

He hesitated before touching her, but then took her small hand into his large one for a brief second. She wore no wedding ring, which made his heart soar. He wondered what that meant; he wondered if Fate was playing a cruel joke. "Call me Dell," he said.

HE WAS THE LARGEST man she'd ever seen. At least six foot six and an easy two hundred pounds, though he looked like he was made of pure muscle under that suede barn coat. His clothes were spattered with mud and his dark hair was too long. The beard gave him a slightly sinister look, but Allison had seen kindness in his brown eyes. He had a large nose in a large, square face that matched the rest of him actually, and he'd just about scared her to death when he'd stopped his truck in the road. She'd realized just how helpless she was at that point, but he'd looked so sorry for her that her fear had disappeared.

Now she was riding in the cab of a pickup truck, her belongings and those of the twins' packed around boxes of groceries under a blue tarp in the bed of the truck.

"I'm really sorry to put you through this much trouble," she said as the rain pelted the windshield. She held the babies awkwardly, and they squirmed a little but otherwise behaved themselves. She hoped it would last.

"Couldn't leave you out there," he said, his voice gruff. He turned the wipers on.

Well, she supposed he couldn't. "Your wife won't mind company?"

"Never been married," he said.

Which was not exactly a surprise. A wife would never let him go to town looking like he'd slept in the barn. And she would have made him shave days ago, too.

He glanced toward her. "Where's your husband?"

"I'm not married, either."

Those dark eyebrows rose, but he looked back at the road, then slowed the truck to make a left-hand turn.

Allison didn't feel like explaining the babies to a stranger. Let him think anything he wanted to think. She didn't want to talk about it. She didn't want to get weepy in front of a stranger, and she didn't want to be reminded that the little children in her arms would someday ask questions. She could answer the ones about their mother, but how could she say, "Your father already had a family"?

"Welcome to the Lazy J," the man stated as they bumped along the road toward a group of buildings clustered together at the base of the foothills. Everything was gray or brown, though some of the fences looked as if they had once been painted white.

"This is really very nice of you."

"No problem." He didn't look at her again. He concentrated on avoiding some of the worse ruts and yet he didn't jerk the truck hard enough to make it difficult to hang on to the children.

"I'm sure it is." She wondered if he ever smiled. He

wouldn't look quite so fierce, she was sure. He parked the truck by the front porch of a grayish one-story house, then came around to Allison's side of the truck and opened her door. He took one of the babies out of Allison's arms and tucked her under the flap of his coat. It was raining harder now, so Allison covered the baby's face with the blanket and made a dash for the front porch. Once there, she flipped open the blanket just as Sophie opened her mouth, ready to scream again.

"It's okay," she assured her little niece. "You're going to be out of those wet pants and have a nice warm bottle and won't have to go in the car seat again, okay?"

Wide blue eyes stared up at her as if she didn't believe a word being said.

"Ma'am?"

She looked up to see Mr. Jones holding open the front door for her. Another giant stood inside the doorway and backed up a step when Allison walked through. This man was dressed in jeans and a plaid work shirt, and he stared at her and past her, to Mr. Jones.

"Hello," she said.

But he still wasn't looking at her.

"Car trouble," Mr. Jones explained to the man. "Found them out on Sourdough Road." The man nodded, and looked down at the baby. "Calvin is my uncle. He's a little hard of hearing, but he reads lips. Just make sure he's looking at you when you talk to him, and speak right up."

"Oh." She smiled at the man, whose gaze dropped to her lips. "Hi. I'm Allison and this is Sophie."

"Hello," Calvin said in a loud voice. He nodded, but he looked disapproving.

"Who am I holding?" Mr. Jones asked.

"Sylvie."

"How can you tell?"

"Sylvie's chin is a little bit pointed, and she has more hair."

Mr. Jones set the baby on a wide brown sofa and went back outside again. Allison turned to Calvin. "Would you hold her for a minute please?"

He nodded, and she handed him the baby and shrugged off her wet jacket. She was glad she'd taken the giant's advice earlier and put it on over her sweater. She'd bet the temperature had dropped ten degrees. She took Sophie back and walked over to the couch. The large living room was warm, though no fire crackled in the fieldstone fireplace. Besides the couch, the room held two dark green recliners, a scarred coffee table, an enormous dark dining table on the far wall, and one large television set. She bet one of those enormous satellite dishes was in the backyard somewhere, too. She felt as if she and the girls had entered a land of giants. Was the ranch filled with oversize cows, too? The thought almost made her laugh out loud, then she wondered if she was simply overtired.

Mr. Jones returned with an armful of their belongings, including the flowered diaper bag, which he had slung over his shoulder.

"It's not fancy," Mr. Jones was saying, looking around his living room. He looked embarrassed, as if he had just realized how bare the room must look. "But at least you're out of the storm."

"It's wonderful, really," she assured him, bending over the babies to unwrap them from their blankets and remove their pink jackets and knit caps. "Is there a place where I can change their diapers?"

"Ah, you can use the spare room."

She tucked one in the crook of each arm and followed Mr. Jones down a dark hallway and past a bedroom, bathroom and office. Calvin followed them as they turned right into a large room that looked as if it hadn't been used in years. A wide double bed, covered with a faded starburst quilt, was centered against the far wall. Two tall dressers matched the golden oak headboard, and the yellowed lace curtains at the windows had seen better days.

"Used to be my mother's room," the giant explained. "There's a bathroom across the hall." He scratched his head. "I don't have any, uh, baby things."

"I had a folding playpen in the trunk of my car. I'll use that." She set the children in the middle of the bed and began to unbutton Sophie's terry-cloth sleeper.

"I'll go get it. I put it in the back of the truck." He put her suitcases on the floor, then set the diaper bag on the bed. He didn't look as if he wanted to be around to witness a double diaper changing.

"Thank you. Again."

"No problem."

And that was the interesting thing, Allison mused. Rescuing a woman and a couple of babies on the side of the road didn't seem to be any kind of a problem at all for Wendell Jones. The man had taken them in without a second thought, though he clearly wasn't accustomed to company. The naked living room and unused bedroom certainly testified to that. Calvin no longer stood in the doorway, having escaped with his nephew the minute he saw that she was going to start changing diapers.

Allison smiled down at Sophie. "I'm not very good at this either, am I?"

Still, she'd had to learn. They were hers to care for now, and she would do anything in the world to do a good job. "Through rain and mud and broken cars," she told the giggling baby. "I will never let you guys down."

"ARE YOU CRAZY?" Calvin's loud voice boomed when Dell entered the kitchen carrying the cooler.

"No." He turned away from his uncle and best friend and set it down on the small table in the corner. He lifted the lid and took out six baby bottles filled with milk.

Calvin waited for him to turn around. "There hasn't been a woman up here for ten years, unless you count the vet's wife, but she didn't come inside the house."

"It's just for the night," Dell assured him, studying the bottles. Who'd have thought that there'd be babies on the Lazy J?

"I'll bet my bag of silver dollars that it's not just for one night. Women are unlucky," the man muttered, wiping his hands on the dish towel. "Where the hell is her husband? A woman shouldn't be traipsing around Wyoming with a pair of babies and no husband."

"I don't think she has one. She said she wasn't married."

Calvin frowned again. "Which is even worse in my book. Did you remember to get coffee or did having a woman in your truck make you stupid?"

"I found her on my way home," Dell explained, unruffled by the old man's grouching. "I'll bring in the mail and the supplies next."

"I'll get them myself," the other man said, heading toward the door to the storage room. He went past the freezer and shelves of canned goods, through the mud-room, and grabbed his coat. "You'd rather go play patty cake or something, and I need the air. Babies and women," he muttered. "What the hell are we gonna do with babies and women?"

He didn't wait for an answer, but slammed the door behind him as he went out into the rainy night. Dell almost smiled. Cal was more scared of females than he was. Cal had come close to getting married once, until the girl changed her mind and broke his heart. Since then he'd been happy to live in the middle of nowhere, cooking for all of the men. It was a position of power, with the built-in right to grumble.

Dell put the bottles in the refrigerator. He'd guess those little girls would be getting hungry, and Allison—Miss Reynolds, that is—would be looking for the kitchen. She wouldn't have any trouble finding it. Calvin had a pot of beef stew on the stove that you could smell for three miles. Fresh loaves of bread lined the counter, and there would be pie for dessert, only Cal would have hidden it somewhere in the pantry. He always hid dessert, though no one on the ranch would have dared touch anything Cal baked without permission.

"Mr. Jones?"

He spun around to see the woman hesitate before entering the kitchen. "Come on in, and call me Dell, ma'am."

"If I do, will you call me Allison instead of ma'am?"

Dell nodded. He could try, but he couldn't promise.

He heard Cal banging things in the pantry. "I put the bottles in the fridge."

"Thanks. If I could have a pan of hot water, I'll heat them up."

Cal came through the door in time to see Dell rummaging in the cabinet for a pan deep enough to hold two bottles. "What are you doing in my kitchen?"

Dell ignored him, which he knew would drive the old crank crazy. "Here," he said, handing a copper-bottomed pot to the woman. "Will this work?"

"Yes, it's perfect." She walked past him to the refrigerator, selected two bottles, and put them in the pan. Then the pan went into the sink and was filled with hot tap water. So far it was pretty much the way they heated up bottles for motherless calves.

Dell caught Cal's eye. "The stew smells good."

"Help yourself. I'm gonna eat with the men."

"You sure?"

"Real sure. And you're on duty. I think it's gonna be busy. Have Rob fill you in." With that, he slammed his hat back on his head and went out the door.

Dell wasn't surprised that he was working tonight. Birthing calves in mud and rain was inevitable. It was the season for calves and mud, after all, and nothing came as a surprise. Except for maybe eight hours of sleep and a day without some kind of emergency.

"I don't think your uncle approves of having company." Allison lifted one of the bottles from the water and tested the temperature on her wrist. Then she took the other one out and dried them both with the dish towel Cal had dropped on the counter. "I didn't mean to chase him out of the house."

"He'll live. Did you get the babies settled?"

"I sure did. Thank you." She smiled again, and his

heart flipped over. "It seems like I'm always thanking you."

He felt his face flush, and hoped the red was hidden by a three-day growth of beard. "You can stop anytime."

"Okay. I'm going to go feed them."

"Supper's ready whenever you're hungry."

"Great. Give me at least half an hour, okay?"

"Take as long as you need to. I've got some work outside." He looked at his watch. "It's already five o'clock. How about you just help yourself whenever you want to? It's calving season." He wondered if she knew what that meant, then decided she wouldn't know. "Dinner isn't anything fancy," he warned her. "Just stew and bread."

"I like stew and bread." With that, she left the kitchen and disappeared around the corner. He knew if he stuck his head into the hall, he would see her hurrying down the hall back to her babies. Those babies were little. When had Allison's boyfriend left her? When he found out he was going to be a father? Or had he died? There'd been a touch of sadness in those eyes, come to think about it. And the babies were young. He hadn't had much experience with kids, but it seemed like when he'd seen Mrs. Petersen's baby, it hadn't been much bigger and the little rascal had been three months old then, because Lucille Palmer had leaned across the counter at Roy's Diner and chucked him under the chin and said, "How old is that little sweetheart?" And Mrs. Petersen had said, "Three months, but he's big for his age."

Then Lucille had winked at him and said, "Just like you, Dell. Big for your age."

And he'd turned red and asked for a refill on his coffee.

Dell thought about those babies and wondered how long Allison had been on her own. She didn't look like she was very good at it. And from the size of their mother, he'd guess Sophie and Sylvie were small for their age. They looked like her, as much as a baby could look like anyone. Fair skinned, wisps of golden hair and big blue eyes meant they'd probably grow up looking like Allison. Lucky girls.

Dell picked up his hat and prepared to go back out into the storm. He should have offered to eat dinner with his guest, but for the life of him he couldn't imagine sitting across the table from her and trying to make conversation for twenty minutes. He didn't know how to entertain a lady, for heaven's sake, and he was too old to learn now. Besides, he told himself, heading through the pantry to the mudroom, then out the door, if Allison didn't have to look at his ugly mug during supper, she'd eat better. He was doing her a favor.

SHE HATED to eat alone. It always felt like she was being punished, which had been her mother's way of teaching her to eat peas. She'd sit at that table, long after Sandy had been excused, and push cold peas around the plate with her fork. Eventually her mother would relent and let her go to her room, but those minutes alone at the dining room table, staring at a small pile of cold peas, had seemed like hours.

But she couldn't expect Mr. Jones—Dell—to entertain her. He was still a little frightening, though he'd gone out of his way to be kind. She figured he wasn't used to having company; it made him uncomfortable, which was something she didn't want to do to someone kind enough to rescue her and her little family from a spring storm and a broken wheel.

The kitchen was empty when she peeked in. The children, their tummies full and their diapers hopefully dry, were sound asleep in the bedroom, leaving Allison with the house to herself. It was the kind of place that she would have been leery of decorating, and yet it would be a challenge. There were stacks of books in corners, and the furniture was old and dark. The place needed brightening without changing its masculine, Western feel. Even the front porch had been filled with stacks of magazines and dust-covered boxes.

She opened cupboards until she found the one that held a stack of white bowls, then she opened drawers until she located the silverware. The room was clean and utilitarian, with almond Formica countertops and vinyl flooring the practical color of dried mud. Allison was ladling stew into a bowl when she heard someone come inside. In a few minutes Dell came into the kitchen. His hair was wet, his face covered with splatters of mud and he was in his stocking feet.

"Bad night," was all he said, attempting to slick his hair from his forehead.

The rain slashed against the window above the sink. "Do you have to go back out?"

"Not for a while. We just got a couple of calves in out of the storm, and Rob's going to ride out again one more time."

She got another bowl down from the shelf. "Do you want to eat now or later?"

"Later?" His bushy eyebrows came together in confusion.

Allison wondered if she'd said something wrong.

"After you clean up," she stammered, hoping she wasn't hurting his feelings. "I didn't want to fix your dinner if it was just going to get cold. I didn't mean you *had* to clean up, or that I expected you to. You're fine just the way you are, being a rancher and all." She took a deep breath and forced herself to stop babbling.

"Oh." He looked down at his mud-spattered clothes. "Guess I don't look too presentable."

"You're fine, really." She started filling the empty bowl. "Sit down and eat with me."

"I'll go wash up."

He left the room and Allison wished she'd kept her big mouth shut. If she wasn't careful, she'd be telling him to shave, cutting his hair and rearranging the living room furniture. The couch would look better facing the fireplace. Allison winced as she carried the bowls of stew to the round table in the corner of the kitchen. She'd never been a person who minded her own business, but now would be an excellent time to begin.

HE MADE SURE he used a lot of soap, because he'd almost scared *himself* just by looking in the mirror. His bedroom was the first room off the hall, a bathroom right beside it. Everything needed painting, he realized. The whole damn house looked like nobody cared.

Which wasn't true. He cared. He just didn't know what to do after the caring part. His parents had been gone for years, and neither one of them had been real interested in what the house looked like. To her dying day, his mother had enjoyed her horses and let the rest take care of itself. He wouldn't be thinking about these things if there wasn't a woman in the house.

He cursed the mirror, scrubbed and dried his face and hands, made an energetic attempt to tame his hair, then returned to the kitchen and his houseguest. Allison had started a pot of coffee and set the table for two people.

"What would you like to drink? Water or milk?" She took two tall glasses from the cupboard beside the sink. She had to stand on her tiptoes to reach.

A shot of whiskey. Then another one. "Water's fine, thanks."

"Okay." She filled the glasses from the faucet, then put them on the table. "I sliced the bread and found the butter. Is there anything else?"

Flowers and wine, he thought. The sound of violins. "No. Looks fine."

"Okay."

Dell waited for her to sit down. He didn't want her to think he didn't have any manners. She sat, tucked a paper napkin in her lap and Dell sat down beside her. The round table was tucked into the corner, so there were only two chairs. He and Cal usually ate standing up, or at different times.

She picked up her spoon, and so did Dell. He tasted Cal's stew and prayed he hadn't gone overboard with the chili peppers this time. Sometimes the man had a mean streak.

"It's very good," Allison Reynolds said. She looked at him as if he was supposed to say something back.

"Cal makes a he—heck of a stew."

"Does he do all the cooking?"

"Yep. He was a cook in the navy before he came back to town, and it just seemed natural for him to keep on doing it here."

"He hasn't always been deaf?"

"No, ma'am. Allison," he corrected himself before she could protest. "An explosion on a ship took most of his hearing."

"Have you lived on the ranch all your life?"

He took a drink of his water. "You sure ask a lot of questions."

"I'm sorry." She held his gaze with her own. "I've been in a car with two babies for three days. It's hard to have a conversation with the radio," she confessed with a little smile that tugged at his heart. "I get tired of talking to myself."

Dell realized he hadn't answered her question about the ranch. "My grandparents homesteaded this ranch.

My parents have been dead for quite a few years now, and I was an only child. I grew up here and I expect I'll grow old here, too."

They ate in silence for another minute or two. It was sure strange to talk to a beautiful woman instead of watching the news or reading the latest edition of *Time* magazine.

"Go ahead," he said, breaking the silence as he buttered a thick slice of Cal's wheat bread. "Ask something else."

"Is this a real cattle ranch?"

"Real?" he echoed, looking at her. The expression in those blue eyes was sincere and interested. "What do you mean by 'real'?"

"I've been driving past ranches and roads to ranches for days. Do you make your living from selling cattle?"

"That and hay."

"Do you like it?"

"Yes." He couldn't imagine doing anything else. His father had made him go to college, but he'd only lasted three semesters. He'd majored in agriculture; he'd wanted to be home.

Allison smiled at him again. "It seems to fit you."

He nodded. Of course it did. He was tall and strong, comfortable in trucks and on horseback. He wouldn't be like any of the other men she'd ever met. He was big and ugly and usually covered in mud that he had to be reminded to wash off.

Dell finished his stew. It wasn't easy having company. Tomorrow he would make sure her car was towed into town, he would urge the mechanic to work overtime to fix it as soon as possible and he'd spend the rest of his day outdoors.

When she left, he would be relieved. He could go

back to eating alone, without having to answer questions or chew with his mouth closed and keep his elbows off the table. Women were different creatures, all right.

"ARE YOU OUT of your mind?"

"No, Mayme. I'm safe, and so are the girls. We could still be on the side of that gravel road, watching the rain hit the windshield," she reminded her friend and lawyer. "And all three of us would be drinking cold formula and crying our heads off."

The older woman's voice was filled with doubt. "The world is full of crazies, Allison. Be careful."

Allison smiled into the telephone receiver. If Mayme ever knew that she was in the Land of the Giants, she'd *really* worry. "He gave me his driver's license and I called the sheriff's office to check on him before the girls and I got in his truck."

She heard the sound of papers being shuffled. "Give me your address and phone number, just so I know where you are."

"We're on the Lazy J ranch, somewhere in the eastern part of Wyoming, off Highway 211." She gave her the phone number. "The man's name is Wendell Jones."

"Wendell?"

"Dell for short. Only he's not."

"Not what?"

"Short." Allison chuckled.

There was a pause. "Have you been drinking?"

"I'm just tired." She fought the urge to giggle. "Riding in a car with twin babies for three days will do that to you."

"You should have taken my advice in the first place and hired someone to go with you."

"I tried. Now I know why no one leapt at the opportunity. Besides, I couldn't fit a box of tissues in that car, never mind another person." And she'd wanted to prove she didn't need Ryan's help. That she didn't need anyone's help. Of course, by taking the wrong turn—not once, but three times—she'd proved she couldn't navigate Wyoming without having to be rescued. "Has Ryan returned the contracts?"

"Yes, but he's been dragging his feet. Maybe he's having second thoughts about letting you go." Allison didn't say anything, so Mayme continued. "I'll transfer the money as soon as you set up an account in Seattle." She sighed. "I'll sleep a lot easier when you're safe and sound and where you're supposed to be."

"I'm fine," Allison reassured her once again. "I couldn't be in a better place."

"Is there a *Mrs*. Rancher?"

"No."

Another silence. "Is Mr., uh, Jones young or old?"

"Middle age, I'd guess. Mid-thirties."

"Hmm... He's one of those bachelor cowboys?" Mayme was fond of reading romance novels, especially the ones set west of the Mississippi. "That could be interesting."

"Not exactly." Allison lowered her voice. "He's kind of shy."

"Ah, the strong, silent type," Mayme declared in a knowing voice.

"I don't know if you'd describe him that way," Allison said. "We had a nice conversation during dinner."

"Let me guess. You asked a million questions and the poor man had no choice but to answer them."

"Well, sort of."

"You should have been a newscaster, Allison, not an interior decorator. You ask more questions than any person I've ever met."

"How else am I going to find out what people want? The more questions I ask, the more I learn about the person. And *then* I can decorate their home. You should see this place, Mayme. I could spend six weeks here fixing it up."

"If your car stays stuck, you might have to."

"Mr. Jones is taking me to town tomorrow," Allison said. "Hopefully the car can be fixed and I'll be on my way." She looked over at the playpen as Sylvie began to fuss. "I have to go. The girls are starting to wake up."

"Give them a kiss for me, and take care of yourself. If your Wyoming cowboy is as tame as you say, maybe a day or two of rest will be good for you."

"Sure," Allison hurried to agree. "I'll call you in a few days."

"Keep me posted," her friend demanded. "And get some sleep."

Allison agreed, and replaced the receiver on the old black phone. Mayme, divorced and childless, had no idea how useless it was to tell the mother of twins to "get some sleep." Allison crossed the room and looked down at the babies. Legally she was their mother, their guardian. She was all they had, and now they were all she had. Somehow the three of them would have to muddle along together. Sylvie lifted her head and started to cry, so Allison lifted her from the makeshift bed and cradled her in her arms.

"Hey, sweetheart, are you going to say hi to me?"

The baby's lips turned down as she stared up at her aunt.

"Haven't decided, have you?" She walked her around the room and gently rocked the child in her arms. The oldest of the twins was the light sleeper; Sophie slept through almost everything unless Sylvie bawled directly in her ear. Allison picked up the phone and decided she'd better return it to the hall. Mr. Jones had gone outside again after dinner, and there had been no one in the house when she'd made the collect call to Mayme. She'd taken advantage of the long cord and taken the phone into the bedroom so she could hear the babies if they woke.

She'd debated earlier about taking a bath and getting ready for bed. It was after eight, and the children usually woke around ten for another feeding. No one had ever told her that motherhood meant waiting all day for a good time to take a shower. She left the bedroom door open so he could hear Sophie if she woke and walked down the empty hallway toward the living room. She wondered if her host was back yet. He'd left after dinner, saying he had a couple of cows missing. She wondered if he counted them every day.

Calvin and Dell were in the kitchen eating pie. They both stood at the counter, their forks raised in midair, as she entered the room.

"Hi," she said, stepping through the doorway. "Sylvie and I are taking a walk."

Calvin's gaze dropped to the tiny baby, then back to Allison's lips. "Want some pie?"

"Thank you. I would love some." She turned to Dell. "Did you find your lost cows?"

He nodded. "They were in a hollow. We got them— and their calves—out of the rain and warmed up." At her questioning look, he added, "A little heat works wonders on the calves."

"Do you always work this late?"

"During calving season, yes."

Calvin carried a plate filled with apple pie over to the table. "Is this where you want your pie?"

"That's fine, thank you." She sat down in a chair off to the side so she wouldn't have her back to the two men, then adjusted Sylvie in her left arm so she could pick up her fork with her right hand. "I'm not used to being waited on."

"How old are they?" Calvin asked, nodding toward the baby.

"Three months," she said. She could see the unspoken questions in the men's eyes. They were wondering what a woman with three-month-old babies was doing driving across Wyoming. "I'm their aunt," she explained.

"Their aunt?" Mr. Jones repeated. He set his empty plate in the sink and refilled his coffee cup. She wondered if he ever slept.

"My sister—" She took a deep breath. "My sister died when they were born. There was no one else to take the children."

"But why are you going all the way to Seattle?"

"That's a long story," Allison hedged. She wasn't going to explain that her boyfriend had refused to help her with the babies, or that she'd sold him her half of the business and, determined to start over with "her" children, accepted her college roommate's offer of a part-time job in Seattle. "Mr. Jones, do you think anyone in town will be able to fix my car tomorrow?"

"Dell," the big man corrected. "Call me Dell."

"Dell," she said, and he smiled just a little bit.

"I don't know about your car. The rain's still coming down real hard, so I don't even know if we'll be able to get to town in the morning. There's not a lot you can do about mud."

"But I can't stay here," she said, taking a bite of pie. "Is there a hotel or motel in town?"

Calvin, reading her lips, shook his head. "Nope. Not this time of year."

"You're welcome to stay here for as long as you need to," Dell said. "Once the rain stops, we'll figure out how to get that car of yours fixed up."

"I hate to put you through all of this trouble."

"No trouble," Dell said, then took a sip of his coffee. "Make yourself at home. Let me know if there's anything you need that you can't find."

Sylvie chose that moment to complain and wave her fists around. "I don't know why she always gets mad when I eat," Allison laughed, shifting the child in her arm. "When she's old enough to pick up a fork she'll think she's in heaven."

"Give her to me," Dell said, crossing the room.

"You're too dirty," the older cowboy said. "I'll take her." With that, he elbowed Dell out of the way and took the child out of Allison's arms.

"Just make sure you support her neck," Allison said when he looked down at her.

"Yes, ma'am." The little girl looked up at him and smiled, which was all Calvin needed to make him smile for the first time since Allison had arrived. "What's this one's name?"

"Sylvie," Dell supplied, surprising Allison with his ability to tell the girls apart. "I have hundreds of cows to remember," he explained. "A couple of little girls isn't so hard."

"Sylvie," Calvin repeated loud enough to make the baby widen her eyes and open her mouth to let out a squeak of protest. "What's the matter with her?"

"You're yelling," Dell told him. "Say something quiet."

"Like what?"

"I don't know. Sing a lullaby or something."

"Don't know any songs like that," Calvin shouted, rocking the baby awkwardly. "I can't carry a tune anymore. Can't tell what I'm singin' half the time."

"Just walk her around a little bit," Allison suggested. "She likes that."

"All right." He carried the baby out of the kitchen and disappeared into the living room. Allison heard him singing "Don't Fence Me In."

Dell didn't waste any time taking up the thread of the conversation. "Why are you traveling alone?"

"I didn't have a choice."

"It's not right," he said, crossing those big arms across his chest.

She wanted to tell him it was none of his business, but that would have been rude. And not necessarily true, since he had rescued her and taken her to his house. She was sleeping in his mother's bed and eating his uncle's apple pie. "Like I said, I didn't have a choice."

"Are you running from someone?" He frowned. "Are you in some kind of trouble?"

"No, nothing like that." She turned away from him and took another bite of pie. She didn't want to explain that grief made a person do strange things, things you'd never dream of doing unless you were desperate to leave pain and sorrow behind. "My life is not that exciting, believe me."

He sat down beside her at the table, and carefully adjusted the chair so his knees wouldn't bump hers. "Guess it was my turn to ask all the questions," he said. Then, "I'm sorry about your sister."

Allison glanced toward him. "Thank you."

"I hope everything works out in Seattle."

"It will," she assured him. *It has to.*

He leaned back in his chair and craned his neck toward the hallway. "I think I hear the other one."

Allison looked at her watch and jumped up. "I didn't realize it was this late," she said. "They're ready for their bottles."

"You have enough food?"

"There's formula in one of the boxes you carried in. I brought enough for the whole trip, though the process has taken a lot longer than I thought it would."

He shook his head as she hurried past him. "Lady, you have no business being on a 'trip' with two little babies." Allison ignored him. She knew he was partly right. Leaving Kansas City had been an act of a desperate woman. She had a job waiting for her, the motel reservations had been made. The Probe had had a tune-up and the car had been packed, the apartment empty and the furniture in storage. And the more everyone said, "Allison, you can't take care of the babies," the more she was determined to do exactly that. It was better for all of them if they started over someplace new.

HE HELPED Allison heat up the bottles and then left the house, leaving Allison holding the quietly whimpering Sophie and Calvin feeding Sylvie. He didn't return for several hours, until he saw the light go off in the bedroom. There were calves to check, of course. And one of the men said there was a black heifer down by the creek, but she'd come up empty. He'd searched through the darkness and the rain until he'd found the calf drowned in the creek, then he'd brought the cow in and gotten her to accept the motherless calf that had arrived at daybreak.

All in all, it had been one hell of a day. The temperature had dropped, but held at thirty-nine. The wind and rain hadn't let up, though, which meant the roads would be thick with mud and he would have his houseguests for another day.

Dell kicked off his boots and stripped off his clothes in the mudroom, then threw them in the pile in front of the washing machine. He wrapped himself in the flannel robe he kept on a hook behind the door and headed into the kitchen. He didn't think he'd run into Allison. The lights were off and the house was quiet, so he walked softly through the kitchen and across the hall to his room. He hoped they would all get a decent night's sleep. Allison had dark circles under her eyes and she'd yawned three times while heating up the baby bottles. She could use some rest. She could use some help. And a husband.

Too bad she wasn't going to stick around. Not that she'd give him a second glance, Dell thought, looking at his ugly mug in the mirror. He would shower now, and shave in the morning so he would look halfway decent. No sense letting the woman think he was some kind of Wyoming wildman.

"MY, DON'T YOU LOOK pretty."

"Shut up." He poured himself a cup of coffee and ignored his uncle's grin.

"You cut yourself, right there under your chin."

Dell faced Calvin and made sure he spoke clearly. "I was tired of looking at myself," he explained. "And it's not such a big cut. Just a nick."

"You coulda bled to death trying to impress the lady."

Dell gave up and went into the living room. He found the remote control, switched on the television and turned it to the weather channel. He kept the volume soft, just to annoy Calvin. And to let Allison and the babies sleep, of course. He went over to the window and looked out into the gray dawn.

"Looks like your new friends won't be goin' nowhere this morning," Calvin stated flatly. Dell turned around as Calvin stepped closer to the television.

"Leave or not, it doesn't matter," he said, then realized Calvin couldn't hear him. He watched as the local weatherman pointed out a nasty front heading south from Canada. The rain wasn't due to let up soon, that was certain.

"Got us another storm coming. Where are you riding today?"

Anything that could happen during calving season usually did. Dell sipped his coffee. "I'll go out through the east meadow, see what's up. Then I have to figure out how to get Allison's Probe into town."

Calvin scoffed. "You looked out the window? The rain hasn't stopped. No way are you going to haul a car down to town today. Or tomorrow, either."

"She's anxious to get that car fixed."

"Yeah, well, women always think they have to have everything they want," Calvin declared. "Doesn't mean they get it."

"I guess," he drawled, not wanting to discuss the whims of women with a man who had no more experience with the creatures than he did. "You don't know a hell of a lot yourself." He felt obliged to point that out.

"Never brought one *home*," Calvin said. "Now that takes bigger balls than those on Marty Kiefer's Hereford bull."

"Didn't have a choice."

Cal shrugged. "Guess not, but it looks like she's not going anywhere for a while. You can't put her in a motel, not with those little babies." Calvin sighed as if he had the weight of the world on his shoulders. "Wouldn't be right."

"I could drive her into Cheyenne."

"Yeah, you could. And what would you do with her car?"

"I see what you mean." The car would be a hundred miles away, in Wells City. He'd have to figure out how to get it to her, or she'd have to figure out how to get it. And she'd have to cart two babies around with her.

"But it's not your problem," Calvin reminded him.

Dell sighed. "I'm the one that brought her home. Which means I'm the one who has to figure out how to get rid of her."

"Women are dangerous."

Dell thought of sitting down at the table with her last night. He had tried to ignore her blue eyes and her neat little body and the way she smiled when she asked him questions. And like a fool he'd shaved this morning.

"Damn right they are."

IT HAD BEEN a good night, Allison realized. The girls had slept from eleven until four, a total of five hours. She'd retrieved the bottles from the refrigerator and heated them in the bathroom sink without making any noise that would wake a sleeping cowboy, and the children had gone back to sleep after having clean diapers and full tummies.

They'd all woken at nine to find the ranch house empty, half a pot of coffee and a dozen cinnamon rolls waiting on the kitchen counter. Allison strapped the babies in their car seats and set them on the table where they could see her while she fixed the day's supply of bottles, drank a cup of coffee and heated two bottles.

She fed them one at a time, in the peaceful kitchen. The rain continued to pound on the roof and against the windows and the wind continued to howl. It was not a day to be outside, but she imagined Dell Jones wouldn't let a little rain bother him. He was the way she'd always pictured cowboys would be in Wyoming: tough and strong, wearing boots and jeans and driving a truck.

"We'd better get used to rain," she told Sylvie, who burped obligingly. "Seattle has lots of rain, I hear. We'll ride the ferry, and go up in the Space Needle, and find a nice little apartment with plenty of room for two cribs." She put Sylvie back in the car seat, then picked up her younger sister and another bottle. "I'll have to get you matching umbrellas," she crooned. "Bright yellow, with pink flowers. How about that?"

Sophie ignored her, latched onto the bottle's nipple and drank as if she hadn't eaten in three weeks. Allison heard the back door open and the sound of boots being stomped against the floor. She turned as Dell hesitated in the doorway of the kitchen. He was clean shaven this morning, which made him look different. He wasn't quite so scary, but his size alone would make any smart person think twice about taking him on. "Good morning."

"Ah, good morning." He took off his hat, and droplets of rain spattered to the floor as he hung it up on a hook. Then, pouring himself a cup of coffee, he leaned against the counter and frowned.

"I'll bet you've been up since dawn," she said, looking at her watch. "I slept late, but so did the girls. It won't take me five minutes to pack, so I'm ready when you are."

"Ready?"

"To go to town."

"Uh, ma'am—Allison, we're not going anywhere today. I can't get your car down to town, not with the storm last night. But I'll try again tomorrow. You're welcome to stay here as long as you need to," the cowboy added.

"Can I take a bus to Cheyenne and stay there until my car is fixed?" She'd looked at the map last night to see how far away from civilization she'd landed.

He shook his head. "Aren't any, least not from here. I'm not sure how often one goes through Wells to Cheyenne, though. Someone at the café might know, but I can't get to town. The storm took out part of the ranch road last night, and it's going to take a few hours to fix it after the rain stops."

Allison considered her options. She had packed their belongings this morning. Before falling asleep, she had worried about the Probe's wheel, then decided that it was a minor problem and could be fixed within hours. How much damage would a pothole do, after all? She'd comforted herself with her options. She'd never considered that a road would be washed out. "I'm really sorry about all of this," she said to her host. "I'm sure you never thought you'd get stuck with all of us for more than a day."

"We'll try again tomorrow. I called Pete at the garage and told him I was bringing a car in for him."

"Do you think it will take long to fix?"

"I don't know. It depends."

"On what?"

"Whether it's the wheel or the axle. And whether he can get the parts he needs."

"Oh." Her heart sank. She hadn't thought about replacement parts. It was a Ford. She'd assumed parts could be found everywhere for a Ford. Sophie finished the bottle and spit it out of her mouth, so Allison tucked her against her shoulder and patted her back. "I know we've been a lot of trouble," she said to the cowboy. He didn't bother to deny it.

"You can't help the rain."

Allison shook her head. "I could have stayed on the right road in the first place, and none of this would have happened."

She noticed he didn't try to make her feel better. Instead he held the plate toward her. "Want a cinnamon roll?"

"Sure." At this rate she'd weigh twenty pounds more by the time she rolled into Seattle because, no matter what Ryan said, she was going to make it on her own. Allison looked past Dell's shoulder toward the kitchen window. Rain streaked down the glass and coated her view of the outside world. She and the children were safe and warm, protected from the harsh Wyoming spring, thanks to one Good Samaritan cowboy named Wendell.

3

"I'D REALLY LIKE to help," Allison insisted, standing by the counter as Calvin assembled the ingredients for bread dough. He ignored her, which meant he couldn't hear her or chose not to. She tapped him on the shoulder, forcing the man to look at her. "Can I do something? The girls are asleep."

"No." He turned away to open a can of yeast.

"I've never baked bread before," she shouted. He turned and nodded.

"Lotta work," was all he said. She watched as he sprinkled yeast into a bowl with water in the bottom and then stirred it gently.

"Can I watch?"

"Guess there's no harm in that."

So she watched the dough-making process. The man's huge hands held a scarred wooden spoon, which he used to mix the flour into the yeast mixture. He turned the mass of sticky dough onto a floured board and proceeded to knead it with gusto.

"Gotta get the air out," he told her.

She was surprised the dough wasn't screaming for mercy, but she leaned against the counter and stayed quiet for as long as she could. Finally, when he set the rounded dough into a clean, greased bowl and covered it with a cloth, she had to ask, "Do you do this every day?"

"What?" He cupped his ear.

She raised her voice to cheerleading decibels. "Do-you-do-this-every-day!"

He nodded. "Just about."

"Lost art!"

"Yes, ma'am." He put the dishes in the sink, washed and dried his hands. Then he gave her a vague smile, went through the pantry to the room where she could see coats hanging, and put on a jacket, hat and gloves. She heard the door slam and watched out the window as he headed toward the barn. Or at least, she assumed it was the barn. There were a lot of buildings behind the ranch house, and it was still raining so hard that she couldn't see much.

Well, so much for conversation. She filled up the sink with soapy water and washed the few dishes Calvin had left. She took her time rinsing and drying, too, and stacked the clean dishes on the other end of the counter. That felt good, so she scrubbed the counters and the table, then wiped them dry.

She checked on the sleeping girls, gathered up the dirty laundry she'd collected in a plastic bag and took it to the kitchen. She'd seen a washer and dryer in the storeroom off the kitchen, and she didn't think the men would mind if she washed baby clothes. The room was lined with shelves laden with large quantities of food, but in the midst of one wall the washer and dryer sat waiting. It didn't take long to find the soap and start a load of wash, and then there was nothing else to do in the quiet house.

Allison left the kitchen and went into the living area. The dining table was a sturdy oak rectangle, but the chairs were missing. Books, lots of them, were stacked against the wall behind the table, between the fireplace and the wall. She went over and examined their bright covers. Mysteries, suspense, techno-thrillers and some Montana history books leaned against the wall. She sat down and flipped through them until she found a medical mystery written by a woman. She didn't really care for serial killer books, but she couldn't afford to be fussy.

She wished Dell would come back inside. He was a quiet man, but at least he answered her questions and didn't seem to mind talking to her. Calvin preferred to ignore the fact that she was there. Allison took the book to the back bedroom and checked on the children again. It was almost lunchtime, but they'd had a busy morning. They'd sat in their little chairs and watched everything that went on in the kitchen. They didn't seem to mind Calvin's loud songs or Dell's awkward manner while he held them. They didn't seem to mind anything except riding in a car for more than thirty minutes at a time. It was going to be a long trip to the west coast, Allison realized, but once they were there everything would be fine. One of her college roommates had promised to help find the "perfect apartment" and the "perfect baby-sitter," too, for when Allison began her new job. Which Carla had insisted would be the "perfect situation."

The perfect situation would have been for Sandy to have survived the car accident, married her lover and lived happily ever after. *I could have been the perfect aunt instead of a definitely less-than-perfect substitute mother*. Allison curled up on the bed, opened the book and was asleep in two minutes.

"HOW LONG?" The two men stopped in the shelter of the calf barn's door and looked out at the rain pelting the mud.

Dell shrugged. "Don't know. After the rain stops I'll have the men work on the road."

"This business of having a woman around is making me crazy."

"Well," Dell drawled, "it's not doing my nerves any good, either."

"Your nerves," Calvin scoffed. "You don't have a nervous bone in your body, son. Never did, not as long as I've known you."

Dell shoved his hands into his pockets. If his uncle only knew that just looking at Allison made his insides tense to the point of pain, he'd laugh until he fell face first into the mud. "Yeah, well, it's not like either one of us is used to having company."

They stood in silence and watched the rain for a few minutes. Behind them, young calves bawled for their mamas and rustled through the hay.

"That's what you need. A woman. You should get to town more."

"I'm not too good at being around women," Dell confessed.

"No reason you should be. You don't have any practice."

"No one to practice on." It wasn't easy to talk to women when you had a face that could scare a grizzly to the other side of the mountain.

"'Cept your houseguest."

"She's the kind of woman you practice *for*."

Cal shrugged. "She'll be gone soon. If you're not gonna get rid of her, you might as well practice talking to her. If you make mistakes, it won't make any difference. By next week, she won't even remember your name."

Dell's heart sank. "Well, that's true, I guess."

"Don't seem right that a man your age doesn't have a lady friend," Calvin commented. "Not that I want you dragging some wife up here." Here the man shook his head. "No, sirree. We don't need any women on the Lazy J, messing with my kitchen and wanting lace tablecloths and pink napkins and making us take off our boots at the back porch and—"

"We take off our boots sometimes," Dell pointed out. "Unless we're just getting coffee and going back out again."

"Mark my words," the older man said. "You get a woman up here and you'll be saying 'please' and 'thank you very much' and keeping your elbows off the table like some Boston greenhorn."

Dell sighed. "There's nothing wrong with having manners."

Calvin turned his collar up against his ears and prepared to cross the yard. "Watch your step, son. And get someone to fix the road. I'm getting a bad feeling in my gut about all of this. It's okay to go to town once in a while for a little female companionship, but it's something else when a woman is walking around my kitchen watching me make bread."

Dell stayed in the shelter of the door and watched Calvin slop through the mud. The sun had to come out eventually, and when it did the roads would be passable, flowers would bloom and the warm Wyoming wind would blow the ruts dry. And Allison and her children would leave and the world would settle back to normal.

He hated "normal."

DELL ATE DINNER with her again. There wasn't any choice and besides, he'd given some thought to that "practice" idea. He'd always thought he'd be one of those men who didn't need or want a steady woman in his life. Of course, his body had protested over celibacy, but a man could get used to a lot of things if he had to. He worked hard and he took a lot of cold showers and he sure as hell didn't watch any of the x-rated channels that came in over the satellite dish.

"So," he tried, "what are you going to do in Seattle?"

"I'm an interior decorator." Allison buttered a cinnamon roll. "I would love to know how to make these."

"Don't you cook?"

"No." Allison smiled at his look of surprise. "Well," she amended. "I'm pretty good at stir fry. But that's just chopping and frying, and following the directions on a seasoning packet."

"Oh." He searched his mind for something else to ask her. Like how she ended up with the two babies who lay on a blanket by the couch. And why she wasn't married. "Do you have a job waiting for you?"

"Yep." She took a bite of the roll and chewed slowly. "A friend of mine offered me a job with her company. Do you think Calvin would give me the recipe, or is that against the rules?"

"The rules?"

"You know. Cook Rules. Never give out your recipes."

"You'd better ask him yourself."

"Why doesn't he eat dinner with you?"

"He likes to eat with the men and he says that I don't have the sense to come inside and eat dinner at six o'clock. He leaves me something to heat up whenever I feel like it."

"It's nice of you to take the time to keep me company," Allison said. "It's been a long day."

"It's a lonely place for a woman," Dell agreed.

She shook her head. "It's the rain. I don't mind the quiet, and the girls are sleeping like little logs. I think they're tired from traveling."

"You still have a long way to go."

"Two days. Maybe three, if we stop early each day. It just depends on how much sleep I can get the night before."

"Going to Seattle must be important."

"Well, we sure couldn't stay in Kansas City."

Dell didn't ask why not. The lovely light vanished from her blue eyes and she looked a little sad. Which meant someone had broken her heart. There was another man, of course. Why wouldn't there be? He finished his last bite of roast beef, pushed his plate aside and wiped his face with his napkin. "I hear that's not a bad town," he said, remembering that he was supposed to keep the conversation going. "I've been to a couple of cattlemen's conferences there."

"I'm looking forward to a change," Allison said. "It will be good for the girls, too."

Dell searched his brain for a safe subject. Life in Kansas City wasn't something to bring up again, and mentioning her sister would just make her feel sad. Those happy little babies were orphans and Allison was alone. They'd already covered the weather and he knew she didn't like the rain. "Calvin might have some cookbooks around here, if you're curious about his recipes."

"Really? You don't think he'd mind?"

Dell decided not to answer that question. His uncle

was as cranky as an old bear about his kitchen. "What he doesn't know won't hurt him."

She smiled. "Maybe I could copy some of them while he's outside."

"Yeah, that's what I was thinking, too." He got up and went over to the cabinet to the right of the stove and opened the door. Inside was a stack of battered cookbooks and an assortment of papers. "I'll bet you can find anything you want in here." He shut the door and poured himself a cup of coffee. "Do you want any?"

"No, thanks. I think that serial killer mystery I'm reading will keep me awake. I borrowed one of your books. You have quite a lot of them."

"I read in the winter. At night."

"You could use some bookcases." She finished her cinnamon roll and wiped her lips. Then she winced. "Sorry. I should mind my own business."

He sat back down at the table. "No, you're right. I had some old ones, but I gave them to the boys in the bunkhouse and never got around to replacing them. I don't spend too much time in the house, so I've kind of let things go."

"The rain stopped," Allison said. "Do you think we'll be able to get the car to town tomorrow? I mean, if you're not busy with something else."

"If it doesn't rain in the night, we should be all right. Most of the calving is over, so I can take the afternoon to go to town. You don't have to go."

"I'd like to, though, if you don't mind."

Mind? He would drive along Main Street with a beautiful woman beside him in the truck. People would talk about it for months. "What about the babies? There's not a lot of room in the cab of the truck for car seats."

"Oh, that's right. I'm not used to thinking about trucks," she said. "I'm not sure what to do about formula and diapers. If the car can be fixed soon, then there isn't a problem. But if it's going to take a few more days, I'm going to need things for the babies."

"You can give me list."

"Thanks. You don't mind?"

"No."

"Thank you." She looked at him and leaned her chin in her hand. "How come you're not married?"

He cleared his throat. "Well, I'm not sure," he lied. He wasn't married because he hadn't found a woman who would look at him twice.

"Don't you even have a girlfriend?"

"No."

She frowned. "I guess there aren't a lot of single women in Wells City."

"No."

"You should get into Cheyenne once in a while. If you learned to line dance, you could—"

"Line dance?"

"Sure. Everyone's doing it in those country-western clubs. You could meet women that way."

He took a gulp of his coffee. He couldn't imagine his size fourteen feet moving across a dance floor. "I don't—"

"I could teach you," she said. "It's easy."

Which holding a conversation with this woman wasn't. "Easy," he repeated, feeling like an idiot. "I don't think so."

"Have you ever tried?"

"Well, no, but—"

"No buts," Allison declared. "I'll teach you to dance in return for towing my car to town."

"You don't owe me anything," Dell tried, starting to feel panic rising within him.

"I have some tapes in my bag. Do you have a cassette player?"

He nodded.

"Good. Maybe later, after I get the girls to bed and you're done with your chores."

"We could play cards," Dell said. "Instead."

"Or do both," Allison declared, standing to clear the table. "Do you think Calvin would mind if I washed up these dishes?"

"No." He would throw a fit, but it didn't matter. If scrubbing plates kept Allison from dancing, she could scrub all night long.

"Good." She left to check on the babies, adjusted their blankets, and talked to them for a minute before she returned to the kitchen. "Did you have more calves today?"

"Yep."

"How many?"

"About sixty today, far as we can tell. All healthy, too." He couldn't keep the satisfaction from his voice.

She smiled. "So we both took care of our babies today."

"I guess you could say that." He helped clear the table, then watched as she filled the sink with soapy water and began to wash the supper dishes. "I could help," he said.

"No way. I'm sure you have lots of other things to do, and I'm happy to be doing something besides fix bottles and change diapers."

"All right." He moved away from the counter and headed toward the coatroom.

"Don't forget," she called after him. "We have a date later on!"

A date. He didn't turn around, for fear she would see the terrified expression in his eyes. "Yes, ma'am," was about all he could manage to say. Within seconds he stepped outside into the darkness to take great gulps of the damp night air.

"Okay," Allison said. "Here we go." She adjusted the volume on the cassette player and stepped into the center of the room. She'd pushed the couch against the far wall and rolled up the rug, which was a definite improvement, she decided. Sylvie and Sophie, wide awake before their ten o'clock feeding, sat in their seats on the couch and watched their aunt walk across the living room toward the tall rancher.

Dell reluctantly stood beside her.

"Here's how it goes. Step, step, forward, kick. See?" She moved two steps to the right, took a step forward, then kicked. "It's in time to the music, one, two, three four. You do it."

"Step, step, front, kick," he repeated without moving an inch.

"Stand beside me and do what I do." She tapped her foot to the music, then started to move. Dell did the "step, step" part, then stopped. Allison turned to look up at him. "What's wrong?"

"I'm not much of a dancer," he said. He looked down at his feet as if they were alien beings.

"You'll be fine. Step, step, front, kick. Remember those four words."

He sighed. "Why am I doing this?"

"So you'll know how, in case you ever want to go dancing."

"Never have before," he muttered, but he smiled down at her when he said it.

"There's a first time for everything. Come on." She moved to the right, and he followed her, then forward and they both kicked in unison. "Very good," Allison told him. "Are you ready for a few more steps?"

"No."

"Sure you are." She explained the next part to him, then rewound the tape to the beginning of the song. "Watch my feet."

"I'm trying to watch yours and mine at the same time."

"Do whatever works," she told him, and had him do it over and over again until he seemed comfortable. When the song ended, she stopped the tape. "There. That wasn't so bad, was it?"

He stared down at her. "What's the name of that dance?"

"I think it's called the Honky Tonk Stomp."

Dell nodded. "Okay. I got it."

"Let's do it again, this time all the way through." She pushed the play button, waited for the count to begin, then started. "Step, step, front and kick."

"Yes, ma'am," Dell said, keeping up with her. He stumbled a couple of times, but made it through to the end of the song without complaining.

"That was great!"

Dell shook his head. "My big feet aren't used to moving this fast."

"Want to try it again?"

He sighed. "You're going to make sure I know how to dance, aren't you?"

"Yep." She put her hands on her hips and smiled at his sad expression. "Don't look so pathetic. You'll have women crawling all over you."

He raised his eyebrows. "What makes you think I don't have women crawling all over me *now*?"

She laughed. "I haven't seen any, Mr. Jones," she teased.

"There could be hundreds of women hiding in the barn, just waiting for me to check on the horses."

Allison started the song again. "They'll all have to wait until I'm finished with you."

He chuckled, and Sylvie started fussing. Allison picked her up, tucked her in her arm and started dancing. "Come on," she urged Dell, who wasn't moving. "We'll run through it again, then add the next steps."

"There's more? How long can the damn dance be?"

Sylvie smiled, and Allison kept moving with the beat of the music to keep the baby content. "Just keep doing the steps until you feel comfortable with them."

He muttered something she didn't hear, because Sophie let out a scream of protest about being left alone on the couch. "Here," she said to Dell. "You dance with Sylvie for a few minutes."

"I can't—" And then Sylvie was in his arms and smiling. "She won't mind?"

"She loves it." Allison scooped up Sophie and returned to the center of the room. "Let's keep going." She led him through the steps, then showed him how to turn to the side and start all over again. When they turned the third time, Calvin was standing in the doorway watching them. His arms were folded on his chest and he looked as if he was witness to insanity. Allison waved to him and kept dancing, but Dell stopped.

Then the song did, too. Allison, out of breath, stopped the tape and adjusted her grip on Sophie.

"Do you want to join us?" she asked the older man in a loud voice.

"No, thank you, miss," Calvin replied, nodding politely to her before turning to his nephew. "Never figured you to be doing the Honky Tonk Stomp."

Dell couldn't hide his surprise. "How'd you know that's what we were doing?"

"I watch the Nashville channel sometimes when I'm cooking. Never tried it, though. Leave that to the younger people." His eyes twinkled and he cleared his throat as he stared at his nephew and the tiny baby in his arms. "And the girlies, too, I reckon."

The "girlies" must be Sophie and Sylvie, Allison decided. "We're all having a good time."

"I just came in for a piece of pie. Don't let me bother you none." He turned and went back into the kitchen as Sylvie squirmed in Dell's arms and started to fuss.

"We have to feed them or dance with them," Allison said. "Which is it going to be?"

"Dance, I guess." He glanced toward the kitchen. "I am never going to hear the end of this."

"Just one more time," she suggested. "Then I'll feed the girls and put them to bed for a while."

"Do they sleep all night?"

"No. Not yet. But they might last till four or five, if I'm lucky." She pushed the button and the music started again. "Remember the steps?"

"Yep. Step, step, front, kick."

"You're going to be a real ladykiller the next time you go to town."

He scowled, which made him look much fiercer than he was, and he missed the kick. "Damnation!"

"But you're going to have to start smiling and look like you're having a good time."

"I'm not."

"Sure you are. Just think, you're dancing with a beautiful girl named Sophie and you're doing fine." Allison watched him out of the corner of her eye. He really was being a good sport, and she felt better than she had in months. Maybe it was the exercise. Or maybe it was because it was the end of a long winter and life was beginning to look a little more cheerful.

WELLS CITY was no city. Population 8,243 said the battered sign at the outskirts of town. Allison sat beside Dell in the truck as they drove down Main Street. They passed a supermarket, then continued on down the street past a bank, hair salon, boot repair shop, drugstore and restaurant on the right, and what looked like some clothing stores and a newspaper office on the left. Allison craned her neck to see. Dell drove through the main part of town to the gas station on the corner of intersecting streets and stopped by the sign that said Automotive Repairs.

"Looks like the men got her down here all right," Dell said, pointing out the car.

Allison saw her Probe parked off to the left of the building. The back tires and the hind bumper were coated in mud, but at least the car was in the care of a mechanic and would be fixed soon. "I hope it wasn't too much trouble for them."

"They didn't mind. I gave them the afternoon off, so they were right pleased to do it. Come on, let's go tell Pete your story." He got out of the truck, and Allison hurried to open her door and follow him across the parking lot. The wind almost took her breath away, but the air wasn't as cold as a couple of days ago.

Pete turned out to be a stocky man a little younger than Dell, wearing greasy overalls and a dark blue baseball cap. "I haven't had a chance to look at your car yet," he said, wiping his hand on a rag. He gave Allison a quick once-over, then glanced at Dell before turning back to Allison. "You got any errands in town?"

"Well..." Allison hesitated. "A few groceries." She didn't want to be away from the babies longer than she absolutely had to. They would probably sleep the entire time, but she didn't like letting them out of her sight. "I really need to get the car fixed as soon as possible, though."

"Okeydoke. Give me half an hour or so. Grab a cup of coffee or somethin' and let me check out that wheel. Front right, right?"

"Right."

"Thanks, Pete," Dell said.

"Yep." He gave Dell a wink, then grinned. "My pleasure."

Allison wondered what the wink was all about, but once again hurried to match Dell's long strides past the gas pumps, past the truck, and across the empty street. "Where are we going?"

"We'll get some coffee," he said, heading toward a place on the opposite corner called Roy's Diner.

"I could get the baby formula while you're having coffee," she offered. What if Calvin had a problem with the girls? They'd already been gone close to an hour, and now another thirty minutes would be added to the time spent away from the ranch. And it was almost forty-five minutes from the ranch to town.

"We can do that on the way out. It's on the way." He

opened the heavy glass door and ushered her inside. The restaurant was small and cozy, with dark blue booths lining the walls and a counter with red-topped stools facing the kitchen. A tall redheaded waitress stared at them when they walked in. She was about thirty, with hair the color of copper swept up in a French twist and secured with bobby pins. Her white waitress uniform revealed a little bit of cleavage and as she looked at Dell, she patted her hair in place with red-painted fingernails.

"Hi, Lucille," Dell said.

"Hey, Dell." She tucked her order pad into her pocket and followed them over to a booth.

Now this was interesting, Allison thought. Maybe the redheaded waitress had a thing for the shy rancher. Allison looked at her and didn't like the amused expression in those green eyes. You'd think Dell had never been in here with a woman before from the way the woman acted. Like she'd seen a ghost.

"What can I get you, Dell?" Lucille ignored Allison.

"Allison?" Dell slid her a plastic menu. "You want coffee and pie?"

"Sure. What kind do you have?" she asked, forcing the waitress to look in her direction.

"Apple, blueberry and Boston Cream. We're out of cherry and peach. The menu's wrong."

"Apple, then. And a cup of coffee." No. Lucille wasn't the woman for Dell. She'd eat him alive in about three days and the poor man wouldn't know what hit him. The ranch house would smell like fingernail polish and hair spray.

"I'll have the same," Dell said, oblivious to Lucille's curious expression.

"I see you have company," Lucille hinted, desperate for information.

Dell frowned. "Allison isn't company. She—"

Allison hurried to finish for him. "Is an old friend." Let the woman think that Dell had a secret life with a mysterious woman. She lowered her voice and gave Lucille a woman-to-woman look. "We're...old friends." She tried to make *old friends* sound sexy and mysterious, and from the way the waitress raised her eyebrows, Allison guessed she'd succeeded.

"For heaven's sake." Lucille turned to Dell. "I'll be right back with your coffee."

Allison ignored Dell's surprised expression and shrugged off her jacket. She looked at her watch. "Do you really think Calvin will hear the girls if they cry?"

"He volunteered to wear his hearing aid. That's a miracle in itself. He says he hates the damn—darn thing."

"I can't believe he offered to take care of them." She couldn't believe she *let* him, but if the mechanic could fix her car she would need to drive it back to the ranch herself. The older man had seemed sincere in his offer to listen for the sleeping babies and to feed them if they woke up hungry. Changing diapers wasn't mentioned.

"Allison, you can't go around letting people think we're living together."

"Do you have a thing for Lucille?"

He looked shocked. "Hell, no. I just don't want people to get the wrong idea."

"I didn't like the way she was acting. As if it was funny that you had a date."

"It's not funny," Dell said. "It's downright hilarious."

"Why?"

*"Why?"* he echoed. "Look at me. I'm not exactly..." He frowned, searching for the words.

"Not exactly what?" she prompted.

"Not what. Who. I was trying to think of the name of the actor who starred in those Lethal Weapon movies."

"Mel Gibson," Allison said. "You're right, you don't look anything at all like Mel Gibson."

Lucille set the mugs on the table and filled them with coffee. "Mel Gibson? Who says Dell doesn't look like Mel Gibson?" She guffawed, and Allison hoped her red hair would turn green the next time she took a shower.

"Dell is more like Robert DeNiro. Only bigger," Allison announced, her teeth gritted. "Don't you agree?"

Lucille acted like Allison had said something funny again. "Robert DeNiro! That's a good one!" She went back to the counter and grabbed two plates of apple pie.

"Enjoy." She slapped them on the table. "When you need a refill on the coffee, just wave."

"Thanks." Dell picked up his fork and looked at Allison. "Aren't you going to eat?"

"I was serious," she insisted. "You do look a little like DeNiro, especially since you shaved."

"Sure," he said, but he didn't sound the least bit convinced. "More like Frankenstein, I think. I'm always asked to be the monster in the junior high's haunted house at Halloween time. They give me a chain saw, with the chain taken out, of course. I make a bunch of little kids scream their heads off."

"That's awful."

He gave her an apologetic look. "I won't do it again, but it raises a lot of money for—"

"No, I mean it's awful that they ask you to be the monster. Just because you're tall."

"And ugly," he reminded her, taking a sip of his coffee. He didn't seem the least bit perturbed.

"You're not ugly."

He ignored her comment. "It's going to be all over town by tomorrow that ol' Dell Jones was in the café eating pie with the most beautiful woman in Wyoming. Folks will be trying to figure that out for a long time to come."

"Good. Let them think what they want." Allison saw Lucille coming toward them and she raised her voice. "You're going to spoil me for other men, Dell," she purred. "Especially after last night. I didn't get much sleep."

Dell choked, prompting Lucille to whack him on the back a few times until he caught his breath.

"Darn," she said, looking at her hand. "I broke a nail."

"I'll take some more coffee," Allison said, giving the woman a polite smile. "I can barely stay awake this afternoon."

"Sure, honey." Lucille gave Dell a sideways glance. "Whatever you say."

"Thanks. Everyone in Wyoming is so nice. Dell always told me I'd love it here."

The waitress hesitated. "You've known Dell long?"

"Long enough."

"You staying for a while?"

Allison shrugged. "Maybe. I just don't know what I'm going to do from one day to the next."

4

"I DON'T KNOW what you're going to do next," Dell muttered once the silent waitress had left their booth and returned to her conversation with Jessie Mc-Dougal. Those two women would talk till the sun turned purple. "But I'm going to drink my coffee now."

"I'm sorry." Allison frowned. "She annoyed me. I didn't mean to embarrass you, really."

He sighed. "It'll be all over town."

"I'm sorry," she repeated. "I honestly don't know what came over me."

She looked so sorrowful that he had to smile a little. "I don't mind. Everyone will wonder how old Dell Jones found himself a woman."

"You're not old."

"Thirty-five."

"You're in the prime of your life," she insisted.

"And you?"

"Twenty-seven."

"You look younger."

"I feel older." She smiled. "I guess motherhood will do that to a person."

He cleared his throat. "There wasn't anyone else besides you to, uh, take the children?"

"No. Their father is already married, with two kids

and a wife who didn't know her husband had been having an office affair with my sister."

Dell didn't know what to say, so he ate another forkful of pie. He didn't know much about office affairs.

"That shocks you," she said. "It shocked me, too."

"Well, I guess people do all sorts of things that surprise me." He managed a smile again. "I should be used to being surprised." Allison had only been in his life for two days, but she'd managed to silence gabby Lucille and fill his quiet house with the sounds of children and music. She'd made him *dance*, for Lord's sake.

Allison set her coffee cup on the table. "Why are you shaking your head?"

"Just thinking," he said.

"About how long you'll have to put up with me, I imagine."

"Well—"

"I guess that depends on what the mechanic says about the car," she said. "I'm trying not to worry, but did you see the way he frowned when I described the sound it made after I hit the pothole? Do you think it's going to take a long time to fix?"

He shrugged, torn between wanting Allison to be happy and yet hoping she'd have to stay a few more days. Or weeks. Or months. He was insane to wish for such torture. "Pete's a real good mechanic. He'll find out what's wrong."

She looked at her watch. "I hope so. Do you think we've given him enough time?"

Dell pushed his half-eaten pie away. He'd had enough, and it sure wasn't as good as Calvin's. He picked up his hat and put it on his head. "Yeah. Let's go."

"I want to get back before the girls wake up."

"Cal's been nursing calves for years," Dell assured her. "A couple of babies needing bottles isn't going to bother him any."

She didn't look convinced. She shrugged her coat on before he could help her, opened her purse and took out her wallet.

"What are you doing?"

"Paying."

"Not in my town, you're not." Dell grabbed his wallet, tossed down a ten dollar bill and glared at his houseguest. "There. Put your money away."

"You're not scaring me with that look," she said. "I think it should be my treat."

"You're not going to pay," he said. "Not when you're with me."

She shoved her wallet into her purse and slung the strap over her shoulder. "I need to do something to repay your hospitality, Dell."

"Why?"

"Because I want to. It's the right thing to do."

He could think of a few "right things to do," but none of them included walking across the street to the gas station and talking about tires.

"HOLD HER real gentlelike," Calvin ordered. He hoped he wasn't talking too loud for the little things. He put the babies in the young cowboy's arms and watched to make sure that Jed had a good grip before he let go.

"How do you tell them apart?"

"Sylvie has a pointy chin." He set the oven timer for five minutes and kept a careful watch on his charges.

"I ain't never held twins before," Jed said, staring down at the babies. "They're real cute."

"Yeah, well, treat 'em gently cuz I'm in charge of

'em," Calvin said. "Dell and the lady went to town to see about her car and left me to watch the girlies."

Jed grinned from ear to ear, and held his arms perfectly still. "How long do I get?"

"Dollar a minute." He squinted at the oven clock. "You paid for five, you have two minutes to go."

"Hello, little girlies," Jed said. "How are y'all doin' today?" He gave Cal a worried look. "It's not extra if you talk to them, is it?"

"Hell, no. They like it." In fact, they were smiling a little bit at the skinny cowboy. Calvin tilted his head to see if they were really looking at Jed or at something past his shoulder. They were such tiny things. He couldn't really believe that they were here on the ranch. Women and babies were pretty scarce at the Lazy J, all right. They were definitely an event, though having babies around all the time would sure get old real fast.

The buzzer made an ugly sound, and the girls' eyes widened. Calvin hurried to shut it off. "Time's up." He turned to the men waiting in the store room. "Who's next?"

Cussy Martin elbowed his way through the crowd. "I am, goddammit."

"Watch your language," Cal cautioned, taking the ten dollar bill from the man. "I don't want the girlies listenin' to that kind of talk."

Cussy flushed bright red. He took off his hat and muttered, "Sorry."

"Sit over there, and try to keep a civil tongue in yer head." He supervised the handing over of the babies from Jed to Cussy, then set the timer for ten minutes.

This was going well. If Dell and the lady stayed away another hour, there'd be a nice chunk of money in the bean pot. He kept a careful eye on the clock, ordered Jed to keep an eye on the road. There was no way he'd hear the truck drive in; Dell had surprised him more than once, and he didn't think his nephew would take kindly to his selling baby-holding time. Not that there was anything wrong with that, Cal figured, but Dell had some strange notions.

And he'd been on the sensitive side lately.

It was all the woman's fault, of course. He hoped that car of hers was fixed up soon. He wasn't sure how much more of this Dell could take. No matter what his nephew said, Calvin had eyes. And he could see that Dell was on his way to falling in love with the little gal with the sweet smile and yellow hair. Hell, Dell had been alone too long, but the boy had no business pining after a city girl with more problems than a three-legged steer.

"PEOPLE ARE SO friendly here." Allison manuevered the shopping cart down the aisle lined with baby food. "Everyone knows you."

"Yeah."

"I'm glad we called Calvin. I feel so much better." She selected twelve cans of concentrated baby formula and put them in the cart. Calvin had assured her that the babies weren't crying, that the bottles were ready to be warmed whenever the girls fussed for their meal, and that nothing whatsoever had gone wrong. The man had sounded almost cheerful, especially after he'd turned the volume up on the telephone receiver and understood who was on the other end of the line. "I've left them with a sitter before," she explained as Dell followed her down the aisle toward the cases of disposable diapers. "And I'll have to **hire s**omeone when

I get to Seattle, of course. But I really don't like leaving them."

"Cal sounded fine."

Allison looked back to see two thirtyish women greet Dell with smiles and friendly hello's. He was certainly a popular man. Everywhere they'd gone this afternoon, from the grocery store to the post office, men and women had gone out of their way to greet him and be introduced to her. It was true what they said about Westerners. She looked at her watch. Pete had asked for more time to call around to see if he could find a part, but he hadn't sounded too optimistic about finding one right away. He'd muttered something about foreign parts on a 1990 Probe, something about a cracked ball bearing, and problems with the axle, but Allison hadn't been able to understand what he was talking about. She'd heard the part where he'd said he could fix it, if he could find the part. That was all that mattered. Maybe she'd have to stay in Wyoming another day, but she'd accepted that already. Staying at the Lazy J couldn't be called a hardship, although she was anxious to get to Seattle and get settled once and for all. All three of them needed a home.

So here she was, in the grocery store in Wells City, while Dell chatted with the local ladies and she filled the cart with baby supplies. She'd buy enough for at least a week, and hope she'd be in Seattle before having to replenish the supply of diapers, formula and baby powder. She would stay at a hotel for a few days, find an apartment, check out the new job, hire a nanny, unpack and—

"Kelly Beatrice," Dell said.

Allison looked up to realize she was being introduced to more of the population of Wyoming. A pretty woman with straight brown hair and green eyes smiled at her. She looked like the kind of woman who rode horses all day.

"Hi," Allison said. "Nice to meet you."

"And I'm June Beck," the other young woman said, shaking her hand. She had lighter hair pulled back into a braid. Both women wore jeans and heavy winter jackets. "I hear you're visiting Dell for a few days."

Allison nodded. Neither woman looked as amused or intensely curious as the waitress, so she answered the question honestly. "Yes. While my car is being fixed."

"That's what Dell said," Kelly replied. "That you had some tough luck on our Wyoming roads."

"I was lucky Dell came along and rescued us."

"Us?" The woman's gaze dropped to the contents of Allison's grocery cart. "You have children?"

"Twins."

"How old?"

"Three months."

June smiled. "I have a six-month-old and a three-year-old, both boys."

"And I have three-year-old twin boys," Kelly said. "So I know what you're going through."

Allison wished she could take Kelly back to the ranch with her. "And you survived it?"

"Yes." The woman chuckled. "But I'm waiting for them to be old enough to go to school. Each phase is something different, and by the time I get used to it, they're on to something else. But it's fun," she added. "And I'm expecting another child in the fall."

"Congratulations," Allison told her. "Another set of twins?"

"Not that I know of."

Dell cleared his throat. "We'd better be getting along."

"It was nice meeting both of you."

"Same here," June said.

"Good luck with the twins," Kelly added.

"Thanks." The women pushed their carts past them and turned at the bottom of the aisle. Allison looked up at Dell. "You must know everyone."

"I grew up here."

"Those women seemed very nice." Allison surveyed the disposable diapers. The selection never ceased to amaze her. Though she'd found it was cheaper to use cloth diapers, she'd opted for the disposable kind during the trip.

"I went to school with both of them."

"Ah," she teased. "Old girlfriends?"

He shook his head and helped her rearrange the shopping cart to fit four boxes of diapers inside. "We'd better get going. You need anything else for the girls?"

"No. That should do it. I won't have to shop again until I reach Seattle." Allison noticed Dell didn't look too happy. Maybe she shouldn't have teased him about old girlfriends. Maybe she shouldn't have flirted with him to make that waitress's mouth fall open. Maybe she shouldn't have disrupted his life in the first place. She would try to fade into the background from now on, she promised herself. Dell was such a nice man, after all. He didn't need her teasing or her questions or her interruptions. "Are you *sure* you don't have a girlfriend?"

"You sure ask a lot of questions about my private life," he muttered.

"Well, everyone keeps looking at us and whispering.

Even in the post office. I can't figure it out, unless they're surprised to see you with another woman."

He sighed, and took the cart from her and headed toward the register at the front of the store. She had trouble keeping up with his long stride. "It's not you," he said once they were in line behind a woman whose toddler screamed for a candy bar. "It's me. No one can believe that I'm here in town with a woman. Not just any woman, either. With a *beautiful* woman."

"I'm not beautiful," she said. "I'm *okay*," she added. "Maybe a six and a half. Or maybe a seven when I'm dressed up and I fix my hair." She smiled to show she was teasing. She expected him to smile back, but he didn't. Dell Jones was way too serious.

"You're a ten," he said with a sigh. "A 'Baywatch' ten. A beauty queen. And you're with the homeliest guy in Wells City. Or even in Wyoming. It's making people laugh."

"No, it's not," she insisted. "I think you're exaggerating. About a lot of things." She looked around and noticed no one looking at them now, except the man bagging the groceries.

The toddler, sniffing back his tears, looked at her and whined, "Can-dee."

"No candy," Allison told him, and he smiled at her.

"See?" Dell observed. "Even the child knows beauty when he sees it."

"Stop it." Allison looked up into his face. He was certainly not a handsome man, or even an attractive one. His nose was too big, his eyebrows too bushy and dark. But the expression in those eyes was sincere. Somehow she knew she could trust him, the way she'd known she could trust him when she'd first seen him. But then, she hadn't been a very good judge of men lately. And trust wasn't high on her list of traits to acquire at this time in her life. Patience, yes. And strong maternal instincts, of course. But trust in one's fellow man—emphasis on the *man*? No way.

"Your turn," he said, gesturing toward the empty conveyor belt. "I'll bring the truck around and meet you out front."

"Okay. Thanks." Allison watched him slip through an empty aisle and leave the store. He was the largest man she'd ever seen, and yet he had such a gentle way about him. She turned back to her groceries. Dell Jones was too nice a man to live alone. She hoped he'd leave his ranch once in a while to go dancing.

"Look," Dell said, not taking his gaze from the road ahead of him. He was afraid that she was crying, and he knew that he couldn't bear to see her tears. "It's not that bad. You're welcome to stay for as long as it takes to find the part." Pete had scratched his head and said he didn't know where the hell he was gonna get an axle to match the Probe's, that it was gonna take a while and no, he didn't have one goldarn guess how long it would take, but he'd do his best.

Dell had felt his heart sink. He was half in love with her already. A few more days and he'd be downright pathetic. A man had his pride and he wanted to hang on to whatever he had left.

"I don't know what else to do," she answered, her voice soft. "If it was just me—"

"But it's not," he said, daring a glance in her direction. She looked upset, but there was no trace of tears. "You have the babies to consider. You can't haul them on a bus to Cheyenne and stay in a motel."

"I know." Her voice still sounded sad. "I shouldn't have left Kansas City."

He wanted to ask why she'd left. He opened his mouth, then closed it. If she wanted to tell him, then she'd tell him.

She did. "I figured I—we—needed a fresh start. I didn't want the girls running into their birthfather as they grew older, and neither did he."

A sharp pain pierced Dell's heart. How was a child to grow up without a father? It didn't seem right. "A child should have a father."

"Yes," Allison agreed. "In a perfect world."

"In any kind of world."

"And if the father doesn't want her? Or them?"

Dell looked over to the woman beside him and shifted the truck into a lower gear as they approached the hill to the ranch. "Then he's not much of a man."

"I'll agree with you there." She looked out the window as rain started dotting the windshield. "When is it spring around here?"

He let her change the subject.

"YOU'RE SURE CHEERFUL," Dell told his uncle after Allison had thanked Calvin for taking care of the babies and bundled them off to her room for a diaper change. "Baby-sitting must agree with you." He expected Cal to deny it, but to his surprise the gruff cowboy just smiled and turned back to slicing bread. Dell raised his voice. "You didn't have any trouble?"

"Now why would I have any trouble?"

Dell shrugged, and filled a glass of water from the faucet. "Taking care of two babies for four hours couldn't have been easy."

It was Cal's turn to shrug as he turned to his

nephew. "They slept most of the time. Till you all decided to come home."

"I told you, we got stuck while Pete tried to find out
where he could buy a part for Allison's car."

"Yep, I heard. She's gonna be here for a while longer,
is she?"

"Yeah. She's pretty upset about her car." He
watched Cal for signs of disapproval and expected the
older man to have a complaint. Calvin turned back to
his loaf of bread and continued to slice. "Well, see if
you can keep her out of my kitchen."

"I'll try."

"I'll take the girlies, though," Cal added. "Next time
you hafta go to town."

"That's real nice of you."

"Nothing nice about it," he stated. "Taking care of
babies is easier than taking care of calves. Cleaner,
too."

"Maybe it wouldn't be so bad to have kids on the
ranch someday."

"Someday?" Cal snorted. "You've gone from learning some silly dance to having babies pretty fast,
haven't you? First, you've gotta get a date." He shook
his head. "I'm telling you, son. Women are trouble."

"Maybe some women," Dell conceded. But then he
thought of Allison's smile and the way she looked in
her jeans. He almost smiled when he remembered the
look on Lucille's face as Allison spoke of being *tired
from last night*. "Not all."

"Yeah?" Cal shot him a sympathetic look. "Guess
you'll have to find out the hard way. With any luck,
Pete will find what he needs to get that girl on her way
before you make a fool of yourself."

"I'm not going to make a fool of myself," Dell insisted. "I'm thirty-five years old."

"Women'll fool you at any age." He stacked the bread on a platter. "I made a pot of chicken tortilla soup. You and the lady can eat anytime you want."

Dell looked at the clock. It was almost five. If he ate now, he could spend the rest of the evening in the barn. "Anything going on outside that I should know about?"

"The calving's winding down, all right. Looks like a pretty good year, considering the weather."

"Good."

"You can spend some time with the ranch accounts," Calvin suggested. "If you're looking for something to do."

"Don't worry," Dell said, taking a long swallow of cold water. "I'm not forgetting I have work to do."

Cal pointed to the pot on the stove. "There's your supper. I'm eating with the boys and we're going to play a little cards."

"Poker?" Dell brightened. Nothing like a good poker game to get his mind off women.

"Gin rummy."

Dell peered into the soup kettle. "How hot did you make it?"

"Not much. You can add your own hot sauce."

"Good."

"Wouldn't want the lady to burn her mouth now, would we?" Calvin winked, but before he headed out the door to the mudroom, he turned to his nephew. "You be careful. I don't want to be picking up the pieces all summer."

"You don't have to worry," Dell replied. And he meant it, of course. He stood alone in the kitchen and decided he would not fall in love with Allison. He was too smart a man to fall in love, especially with a woman who was obviously so beautiful. A woman with babies. A woman heading for Seattle to start a new job. He would avoid her from now on, he promised himself. And he would start right after dinner.

ALLISON DIDN'T KNOW what was the matter with the girls. They'd slept like little angels until two o'clock. First one and then the other woke up and began to fuss. Allison didn't feed them right away, since they'd had their bottles around midnight. It wasn't time for another feeding, but the two girls were complaining about something, but Allison couldn't figure out why they were so upset. They'd been sleeping longer this past week or so, letting Allison sleep from midnight until five or six in the morning. But tonight Sophie and Sylive wanted to be held, and they wanted to be walked. They wanted to look around the room from the vantage point of their aunt's arms. They made it clear that they didn't want to be put down.

So Allison, afraid their cries would wake Dell, walked the babies around the bedroom until she thought her arms would drop from her shoulders. Whenever she tried to put them back to bed in their little playpen, they would lift their heads and begin to cry. Their pitiful cries sounded as loud as fire alarms in the darkness, so Allison would pick them up again and, with a child tucked in each arm, walk around the room for a while longer.

"Are you hungry?" she asked Sophie, whose left side of her mouth lifted into a tentative smile. Sylvie matched her sister's expression, making the two of them look identical in the dim light. Neither child looked sleepy or in pain. "Okay," she told the girls. "We'll try having a middle-of-the-night snack and see what happens. You two wait here while I get your bottles, all right?"

It wasn't all right, which the girls made perfectly clear the minute Allison set them down in their bed. They screamed once again, and Allison knew that within minutes she would be guilty of waking their host. It wasn't right to wake a man who worked eighteen hours a day. He'd gone outside after dinner and hadn't returned before she'd gone to bed. The house had been quiet at midnight, so she'd assumed he was either asleep or working in the barn. Through the kitchen windows, she'd seen lights in some of the distant outbuildings.

She would have to tiptoe to the kitchen and warm up the bottles without waking Dell, which wasn't going to be easy with an armload of babies. Allison opened her bedroom door and saw a faint glow of light from the other end of the house, which meant that someone had left a light on in the kitchen. She made her way along the dim hall, past Dell's closed bedroom door, and into the kitchen where the light over the sink illuminated the room.

Allison settled the girls in their car seats, then lifted them onto the kitchen table. "Please," she told them. "Be good girls. You don't want to wake up Mr. Jones, do you?"

Sylvie glared at her and let out a howl of complaint, which Sophie immediately copied. Allison hurried to the refrigerator, grabbed the bottles, stuck them in a pan of hot water and returned to the girls. "You have to stop," she told them, trying to make her voice sound as soothing as possible. "You're making too much noise. Hush, now."

They didn't want to hush. They wanted to cry, which they continued to do, until Allison retrieved the bottles, tested the temperature, and attempted to give the babies their unscheduled feeding.

"What the hel—heck is going on out here?" Dell stood in the entrance of the kitchen and stared at the three of them. The babies twisted their necks to see who had arrived and let the formula drip from the corners of their mouths before they began to scream again. Allison set the bottles on the table and tried to explain. Which wasn't easy, considering that Dell was only half dressed. He wore no shirt, so his wide chest was bare and covered with dark hair. He'd zipped his jeans but forgotten to fasten the snap, and his large feet were bare. The poor man looked half-asleep. And totally sexy, which surprised her.

"They're not happy tonight," Allison explained, conscious of her thin flannel nightgown. It came to her ankles and covered her arms, but the neckline was scooped low and edged with lace. She would be all right if she didn't bend over.

"I can hear that." He stepped into the room and spoke to the girls. "Are you two giving your momma a bad time?"

"They know I'm not their mother."

"You're their mother now," he pointed out. He unfastened the safety belt across Sophie and scooped her into his arms. She promptly stopped crying, but her sister continued to complain. Allison soon had the baby in her arms, which seemed to make her happy.

"It's like they just want to be held."

Allison looked at him with surprise. "Do you think so?"

"Well, sure seems that way. Try putting her down and see what happens." Sure enough, Allison made a motion to tuck Sophie in her seat and the little girl immediately screwed her mouth to howl.

"I don't understand. They've never acted this way before. And they'd just started sleeping longer in the night." Allison sank into one of the wooden chairs and cradled the baby in her arms. "I thought we were all going to start getting some rest."

"You are," Dell said, his voice soft. "Starting now. Give me Sophie and go to bed."

She stared up at him. "I can't do that."

"Why not?"

"You've taken us in, which doesn't mean you have to take care of us twenty-four hours a day."

"I didn't say I *had* to. I'm offering. How long has it been since you've slept through the night?"

Allison couldn't remember. She'd taken the children when Sandy had died and the hospital had pronounced them well enough to leave the nursery. Ryan had complained about the noise, the interrupted nights, the mess in the apartment, until Allison had moved into the babies' room to sleep. "More than three months."

"It shows."

Which wasn't polite of him to point out. "I'm getting used to it. They say it can't last forever."

"Go to bed, Allison." His voice was low and quiet. "I'll sit up with them for a while, and when they go to sleep I'll bring them in to you. That is, if you don't mind."

Mind? She wished he'd put a shirt on. That enormous chest was disconcerting, especially when he walked toward her and held his empty arm out for the second baby. Allison stood and put Sophie in the crook of his arm. Her fingertips brushed Dell's skin and a small part of the crispy mat of dark hair that covered a chest the size of a king-size bed.

She shouldn't be thinking about beds, she reminded herself as she withdrew her hand from further contact with Dell's warm skin. She folded her arms across her chest and surveyed the two babies who gurgled their contentment.

"I'll see if they want to eat," Dell said. "They can't stay awake forever."

"And neither should you."

He shrugged. "I'm used to being up half the night. You don't have to worry."

"I worry about everything," she confessed. "I can't seem to stop."

"Get some rest." Dell backed up a few steps so she could walk toward the doorway. "The girlies and I will be fine."

She believed him, though she wondered why she took his word so easily. "Thank you. I'm always thanking you for something."

"You don't have to. It's not as if I didn't offer."

"You've offered too much."

He shook his head. "Shut up and go to bed."

Allison smiled and left the room. She walked slowly down the hall, giving Dell time to change his mind about taking care of the children. She wanted to hear if they screamed when she left the room, in which case she'd hurry back to the kitchen. But they were quiet, and Allison left her bedroom door open to hear them cry, to hear Dell call if he needed her.

She was asleep in minutes. Almost before she could wonder at the strange sensation touching Dell's skin had caused.

5

HE COULD STILL FEEL the touch of Allison's fingers against his skin, even after an hour of carrying the babies around the living room. His plan to avoid her hadn't lasted long. Here he was, half-dizzy with desire, walking around the house in the middle of night with an armload of babies. Allison had touched him. Unintentionally, of course. She had put the babies in his arms and couldn't avoid touching him. He understood that, but knowing it was accidental hadn't lessened the impact of having those gentle fingers sweep over his heart.

His little charges had finally closed their eyes, but Dell didn't stop walking until he was certain they were really asleep and not just relaxing. When he put them to bed, he wanted them to stay asleep so Allison could rest. Dell stopped walking, but the babies didn't open their eyes, so he walked slowly down the hall toward Allison's room.

*Allison's room.* He thought of it as that already. Long after she'd driven away, he would most likely think of it as Allison's room. The door was open, but he hesitated before stepping inside. He could hear her slight, rhythmic breathing and smelled baby powder and the faintest floral perfume as he passed the dresser and headed to the playpen. He steeled his heart against the intriguing scent of a sleeping woman only three feet away. There was enough light from the kitchen to see that Allison lay curled on her side facing the playpen. He would give a million dollars if she was his, if he had the right to join her in the double bed. She would be warm and sweet. She would be welcoming to a beat-up cowboy. He probably didn't look too bad in the dark, and his body was big, but all muscle. He wondered if she would think he was too big, too hairy.

There was no reason to wonder, of course. She wasn't staying. She wasn't his. She was his guest, and she would never know that he harbored a secret longing to take her in his arms. He took a deep breath and turned away, toward the playpen.

Now here, dammit, was an unexpectedly tricky part. How was he supposed to put one baby down without letting go of the other one? It was a long way down to the bottom of the playpen. He considered bending over and releasing one child, then the other, but rejected that idea as too risky. What if they woke up? Or worse, hurt themselves? He turned toward the bed and swallowed hard. He could leave one baby on the bed with Allison while he positioned her sister on the playpen's mattress, but that would risk Allison waking up and thinking, well, thinking there was a cowboy touching her bed.

Hell and damnation. He had no choice but to bend over and ease Sophie onto the mattress, near the little ridge made by Allison's feet and not too close to the edge of the bed. Then he turned and carefully set Sylvie on her back in the playpen before hurrying back to the bed for Sophie.

"Dell?" His name was a whisper in the darkness that sent warmth surrounding his heart. He froze, and Allison smiled sleepily. "Is everything okay?"

"Yeah. It's fine," he assured her, resisting the urge to kiss her forehead and tuck the yellow quilt over her shoulder. While he grappled with how to explain why he was standing by her bed, she closed her eyes and went back to sleep. Dell wasted no time getting out of there. The baby's eyelids fluttered as he scooped her into his arms, but she didn't wake when he bent over and lay her beside her sister. He covered them both with a pink blanket and watched them for a few moments until he was certain they weren't going to wake up and holler again. Then he left, shutting the door soundlessly behind him before hurrying down the hall to the kitchen and a shot of some rare kind of Scotch he'd won at last year's May Day dance.

He sat in the semidarkness, in the battered recliner, and thought about his home and his life while he drank the kind of whiskey a man saved for special occasions. It was an occasion, he decided, thinking hard about how he wanted the rest of his life to be. He didn't want to be alone anymore. He liked the smell of baby powder. He thought the sound of a sleeping woman's gentle breathing was music, and the touch of her fingers against his chest had made him almost choke with surprise and longing. He would keep her if he could, though there wasn't much to offer her in the way of luxury and excitement. The Lazy J was a good ranch, one hell of a good ranch, he amended. The land had served his family and himself well; they'd preserved their share of heaven, all right. But the house was plain and stark, the furnishings old, the fancy things that would appeal to a woman nonexistent. Stacks of books and magazines weren't exactly decorations, though he and Cal sure hadn't minded living with reading material within easy reach. Dell sat and thought some more.

If he were a woman, what would he want? He reached down and set his empty glass on the floor, then reached for the JCPenney catalog, the big one that was underneath the stack of *Outdoor Life* and *Sports Illustrated*. He ought to be able to find something in those pages that would give him some answers.

SHE STUDIED *All About Babies* the next morning, while she drank coffee in the kitchen, but she couldn't find anything that explained why babies would fuss and cry at night if they weren't teething, didn't have colic pains, or hadn't been asleep all day.

Calvin, his hearing aid in place, cut up meat for a stew and fussed over dough in a thick pottery bowl before turning to look at Allison's reading material. "You studying?"

Allison nodded and flipped to the section called "Setting Schedules." "I don't know why the girls were awake most of last night. It was as if they just wanted to be held."

"Maybe they were lonesome."

She looked up at him and, hoping the hearing aid worked, raised her voice a little. "Exactly. They wanted to be held and talked to and played with, as if it was the middle of the afternoon." She yawned. "It was very strange."

Cal shrugged. "Guess they like company."

"In the middle of the night?" She shook her head and scanned the paragraphs describing a typical baby's routine. None of this was new to her. "At this rate, they'll be two years old before any of us sleep eight hours in a row." She glanced out the window, where blue sky and spring sun waited. "I'll take them for a walk today. The fresh air will be good for them."

"How?"

"Good question. I don't suppose I can get the stroller to work on dirt."

"Not dirt," Calvin said. "Mud."

"Maybe we'll sit on the front porch, then."

He nodded. "I'll show you a better place. More sun. After I get this stew fixed."

Calvin was as good as his word, for an hour later found them heading out of the back door toward a set of buildings on the other side of a muddy yard where several roads crisscrossed. The girls had been fed, washed and dressed, then tucked into identical infant sleeping bags for their outdoors adventure. Allison, with Sylvie in her arms, followed Cal and Sophie across a wide field of mud toward a neat gathering of outbuildings. One housed a screened porch that faced southeast, judging from the way the sun's rays touched the windows. Allison carried a thick blanket she'd found in the closet and, once on the porch, laid it like a mattress pad on the floor and let the girls lie on their backs and kick.

"What're they lookin' at?" Calvin cracked open one of the windows and let in a breath of spring air.

Allison followed Sophie's gaze as she tried to reach for a sunbeam that crossed her chest. "The sunshine, I think. They're at the age now where they're noticing things and want to try to touch them."

"Huh," the older man said, sitting down in a well-worn wooden rocker. He gestured toward its mate. "You'd better sit down. You're looking a little peaked."

"Actually, I feel fine. Dell helped—" Allison stopped, not wanting Calvin to know that she'd kept his overworked nephew awake last night. She glanced at the old cowboy, but he paid no attention to her, so she assumed he didn't hear what she'd said. His attention was fixed on the way the girls flailed about on their blanket.

He turned to Allison and frowned. "They warm enough?"

"I think so. We're out of the wind, and the sun is shining." She looked around the porch. The wooden floor had been swept clean, and the windows that lined the upper half of the walls gleamed. "What building is this?"

"Number two bunkhouse. Holds four men."

"How many bunkhouses are there?"

"Used to be four. Now we just use number two and three. Number one has the tack, and number four is for summer, for the hay crew."

"You all work so hard."

"Dell most of all," Cal added. "Can't get that boy to slow down."

"Maybe he should take a vacation."

Calvin chuckled. "That'll be the day. He loves this place, it's in his blood, and there ain't nothin' that's gonna keep him from it for very long."

Allison wished she had that feeling about where she lived. "He sure works hard."

"Yep. He got that from his father. Never saw such a hard-workin' man in my entire life. My brother could do a day's work in a morning and keep goin'. Guess that's why the old place is still doin' okay after all these years."

Allison wondered what "doin' okay" meant. She'd assumed the sparse interior of the ranch house meant that Dell didn't have the extra money for furniture and the luxuries that would make the place look, well, homey. He must have put all his profits, if there were any, back into buying cattle and land.

"Well, speak of the devil," the old man muttered. Allison looked up to see Dell riding toward the bunkhouse. He wore an unzipped green down vest over his flannel shirt and his dark hat was tugged low on his forehead and gave him a sinister look. The horse was a massive black animal that looked like a replica of the black stallion in the books she used to read when she was nine. She watched as Dell, unsmiling, dismounted, tied his horse to the railing and pushed the door open to the porch.

"Ma'am," he said, tipping his hat.

"Hi." She smiled, glad to see he didn't look tired after taking care of the babies last night. His gaze dropped to the floor.

"They okay down there?"

"Right as rain," Calvin answered. "It's good for them to have a change of scenery and some fresh Wyoming air."

"How would you know that?" his nephew asked.

Cal jumped. "You don't have to yell. I've got the hearing aid on this mornin'."

"Sorry." He glanced at Allison and his expression lightened, which made her smile once again. He didn't look like an outlaw when he wore that almost-smiling look.

"It's a beautiful morning," she said.

He nodded.

Calvin leaned forward. "You should take Miss Allison for a ride." He turned to Allison. "You ride, don't you?"

"Not exactly. I mean, not since I was twelve."

The old man nodded and turned to Dell. "Good

enough. I'll stay here with the girlies and we'll enjoy the sunshine."

She wasn't sure about interrupting Dell's work and searched for an excuse. "They're going to need to have bottles in about two hours."

"Yep. I'll get one of the boys to help me carry 'em back to the house."

"Cussy is in the main barn," Dell said. "I'll tell him to listen for you."

"I can ring the old dinner bell."

"Yeah. Good idea." He turned to Allison. "You up for a ride?"

"If it's not any trouble. And if you give me a horse about half the size of yours." She wasn't kidding, either. She didn't want to be sitting six feet off the ground if she fell off.

"Done."

Allison stood and looked down at her leather boots. They weren't cowboy boots, but they had a little bit of a heel. She wore jeans and a pale blue sweatshirt. "Will I be warm enough?"

"I'll get you a jacket," he said, disappearing into the bunkhouse for a minute. He returned with a thick brown barn jacket, which he handed to her. "It gets cold out there in the wind."

"Thank you." She shrugged it on and folded the sleeves back. She smiled down at the babies and told them to behave. They looked at her with identical curious expressions and both smiled at the same time. "I'll be back soon," she promised everyone.

"Take your time," the older man said, leaning back in the rocking chair. "We're just gonna sit out here and enjoy the sun."

Dell held the door open for her, and she walked out into the sunshine.

"Never known Cal to be so domestic," the cowboy muttered behind her. "Come on," he said, untying the big horse. "Let's go find you a mount."

"This is a lot of trouble, isn't it?"

He stopped and looked down at her, surprise lighting his dark eyes. "Why would it be any trouble?"

"But your work—"

"Can wait," he finished. "I should have realized you'd like to see some of the Lazy J while you're here."

"I've never been on a cattle ranch before," she admitted, falling into step beside him. She had to hurry to keep up with his long strides as they headed toward a big red barn. Several cowboys were grouped around the big double doors in the center of the building. When they saw them approach, they straightened and stared.

"You can meet some of the men," Dell said. "And we'll find you a horse." He led her over to four men who definitely looked as if they made their living outdoors. Dell introduced them as Cussy, Jed, Sam, and Rob; the men tipped their hats and looked curiously at her.

"You get that car fixed, ma'am?" the tallest one asked.

"Not yet. I guess it's going to take a few days to find a part."

"You want to saddle up Gertrude for the lady?"

The balding man called Jed shook his head. "That old mare is half dead, boss. Like riding a tree stump."

"Do it," Dell said. "The lady wants a quiet mount." The cowboy shrugged and disappeared into the barn. Dell turned to the others. "Cussy, when you get through out here, listen for Cal. He's got the babies on the porch on Bunk Two. He might need a hand."

"Cal's got the girlies again?" The thick-set man grinned. "How'd you manage that?"

Dell shrugged. "He just seems to like 'em."

Cussy chuckled. "Damned right, he does. Why, he's—"

Another cowhand elbowed him in the ribs. "Watch your mouth, Cuss. You wouldn't want to say anything to offend the lady, would you?"

Cussy paled. "No, course not."

Dell ignored them, instead turning to Allison and surveying her outfit. "You look close enough to a cow-girl."

She brightened. "You think so?"

"Sure." The horse was brought out for her, and Allison eyed the animal with some relief. She was a medium shade of brown, with a black mane and tail, and Allison figured if horses could yawn, this sleepy-looking horse would certainly do so. "Climb on," Dell said, "and I'll fix the stirrups."

She remembered this part, left foot in the stirrup, then grab the saddle horn and swing the right leg over. At least, that was the way it was supposed to work. Luckily the brown mare was small, and Allison mounted on the second try. Dell held the mare's reins while his own horse waited patiently behind him. She grasped the reins and looked down at Dell. "Okay, so far, so good. Now what?"

"Just stay in the saddle and keep up." He adjusted the stirrups, checked the cinch, patted the little mare's neck and then mounted his own horse. "You know how to ride Western, don't you?"

"Yes. Right rein on the neck to go left, left rein to go right."

He nodded and swung his horse around. "Come on," he called, giving his horse a nudge with his heels. "It's time you saw the Lazy J."

"Why do you call it the Lazy J?" She noticed the remaining cowboys got out of her way fast enough.

Dell shrugged. "The brand is a leaning J in a box. I guess my grandfather thought that was as good a reason as any to name the place the Lazy J." He led her toward the bunkhouse. "We'd better check on the babies before we get going."

Allison followed him to the porch, where he dismounted, talked to Calvin, and returned to Allison, who didn't want to try to get down from the horse and get up on her again. "Is everything okay?"

"Yep. Sylvie's asleep and Sophie's not far behind. Cal's reading a magazine and acting like he's retired." Dell chuckled. "Lord only knows what we'll eat for dinner tonight."

"Stew. I watched him make it this morning." Allison urged her horse to keep up with Dell's, but the mare was clearly interested in walking slowly. Which was fine, too, Allison conceded, feeling safe and comfortable as they rode west toward the foothills of the Rocky Mountains. "Where are we going?"

"To check on the new calves. Thought you'd like to see some of 'em."

"I'd like that." She realized she'd like just about anything right now, whether it was looking at calves or breathing in fresh spring air or gazing at the distant dark mountains. She loved those babies, but for the moment it was wonderful to take a break from their care. Yesterday she'd worried about the car, buying supplies, getting back to the ranch before Calvin had problems with the children, but today she was outdoors. The babies were content; their baby-sitter wore a hearing aid. Sandy would have loved to have seen this, Allison thought. A familiar stab of pain lanced through her heart. Thinking of Sandy always hurt. She wondered if it always would, and hoped that somehow, as everyone promised, time would lessen the pain. Ryan had urged her to "get a grip on herself," while well-meaning friends gently questioned the wisdom of keeping the children to raise.

"Allison?"

She looked over at her host. "Yes?"

"I was just asking if you were doing all right with Gertrude."

She wondered if all cowboys were gentle giants like the one who had rescued her. "I'm fine."

Dell nodded, looking as if he believed her, and pointed to a mountain range off to the west. "The ranch runs halfway up those foothills," he told her. "We summer a herd of cattle up there."

"This must be a very large ranch."

"One of the biggest in the county."

"Calvin says you work too hard." She urged Gertrude to fall in beside Dell's black horse.

He gave her a curious look. "What else is there to do?" Then he cleared his throat. "I like the work. It's all I know."

Allison looked around as they rounded a hill. Cows and calves dotted the brown landscape under a pale blue sky, a view that took her breath away. She'd driven past a few places like this and seen them from the interstate, but riding horseback through this country was a much different experience. They rode together for more than an hour before Dell turned his horse in the direction of the ranch buildings. Allison, relaxed and comfortable on Gertrude, surveyed the cows and calves that dotted the pastures. "You're a lucky man," she told him.

He nodded slightly. "In some ways."

In many ways, Allison wanted to say. He knew who he was and where he belonged. There was a lot to be said for having a home. As soon as she reached Seattle, she was going to make sure that she and the girls had one of their own.

"I COULD DRIVE out there and get you," Mayme suggested, and Allison tilted the telephone receiver away from her ear a little. "I could bring you back here, where you belong, and you could forget all this nonsense."

"I appreciate that," Allison replied. "But everything is fine, really. I'm sure it won't take long to fix—"

"How long exactly? Do you know?"

"No. The mechanic is going to call when he knows where he can get a part."

"Let me bring you home," Mayme pleaded. "You and the babies have no business staying with strangers. I could be out there in a couple of days. I'll rent one of those horribly domestic minivans."

"That's quite an offer." Allison laughed. She stood at the kitchen counter and looked down at her dusty jeans and mud-covered boots. Mayme wouldn't recognize her; she'd always prided herself on wearing unusual, colorful clothes. People expected a decorator to be dressed in fashionable and "artsy" clothing. Now she needed a shower and clean clothes, and those clothes would be another pair of jeans and a sweatshirt that would soon have formula dribbled on the shoulders.

"I'd do it. For you." Mayme's tone turned pleading. "Please, Allison. Reconsider this whole idea. Ryan was never happy about your leaving the business, or leaving him, for that matter. I'm sure you two could work something out."

The smile faded from Allison's face. Dell passed her as he stepped into the kitchen and gave her a concerned look. "He made his feelings clear."

"People change."

"Not that much, they don't," Allison said, not wanting to prolong the conversation. Dell might need to use the phone, or the babies could be fussing and she wouldn't be able to hear them. "Look, I have to go."

"I called your friend in Seattle and told her you'd been delayed."

"Thanks. She wasn't too worried, was she?"

"We're *all* worried." Mayme sighed. "I hope your cowboy is taking good care of you and the girls."

"We're fine. Spoiled, even." She smiled across the room when Dell looked at her, and he looked surprised.

"Call me if you need me," her friend urged.

"I will. Bye." Allison hung up the phone and turned to Dell. "I called my friend back home again. She's worried about me."

He nodded. "I can understand that."

"You can?"

"Yeah. You don't get enough rest."

"That part's getting a little better. Thanks again for the help last night."

"It was nothing." But he didn't sound convincing.

"It was," she insisted. "Let's hope they sleep a little better tonight."

"Yeah," Dell said, smiling a little. "Let's hope we all do."

Allison smiled in return. "Thanks again for the ride this morning. The girls have been sleeping all afternoon. I might even have time to clean up before supper."

He looked at his watch. "Take your time. I just came in for a cup of coffee and then I'm heading back out until six or seven."

"I'll just go ahead and eat by myself then?" She tried hard to hide her disappointment. She'd enjoyed their meals together, and she had a lot of questions about the ranch now that she'd seen some of it.

"Uh, yeah. I mean, no." He turned away from her and poured coffee into a stained white mug. "I'll make sure to come in by, what, six-thirty?"

"Okay. I'm going to clean up and do some laundry."

"Get some rest instead," he said, taking a sip of coffee. "You look tired."

"I have two babies," she declared, feeling defensive. "How else should I look?"

He almost smiled again. "I meant no offense."

Allison sighed. "Sorry. Maybe you're right about resting."

"How much longer will they sleep?"

"Maybe an hour. More, if I'm lucky." She smiled. "I'm learning that mothers of babies have to choose between taking showers and taking naps."

Dell leaned against the counter and finished his coffee. "Me or Calvin will watch 'em later, while you clean up." He put his mug in the sink and moved toward the door. He had to pass her on his way out of the kitchen, so he paused and tipped his hat. "See you at supper," he said.

"Six-thirty," she agreed, watching him leave the room. She heard the door bang shut a few seconds later, so she went to the kitchen window and watched Dell cross the muddy expanse between the house and the barns. There were sheds for the calves and bunk-houses for the men, and corrals for the livestock. It looked like a small town, especially when she'd seen it from the back of Gertrude. This Wyoming ranch was like no place she'd ever seen before, and she felt oddly comfortable here in the old ranch house. She thought she would have minded the isolation, but there were people outside. And Dell had told her that two of the summer hands were married, and their wives and children would be returning to the ranch soon. That's what a man like Dell needed, a wife and children. She couldn't imagine why he wasn't married.

DELL WHISTLED as he double-checked the calves. It was amazing what a little bit of warmth could do for them. They perked right up after a few hours out of the wind. He was pleased with the day. Allison had managed to stay on the old mare—anyone would, though—and she'd seemed to have a pretty good time riding around the lower sections. They'd ridden for more than an hour and he'd enjoyed every damn minute, too, until he'd realized the babies would be needing her and turned the horses toward home. Maybe they could do that again. Calvin had surprised him and turned into a damn good baby-sitter. When they'd ridden toward Bunkhouse Two, he'd seen cowboys clustered near the door. No doubt they were teasing the hell out of Cal-vin. It wasn't often the men had a chance to heckle the grouchy cook and get away with it. Cal would most likely put extra pepper in the meatloaf or cook tomorrow's roast so it tasted like boot leather.

He talked to the men and organized tomorrow's chores. "I need someone to take a truck to Cheyenne in the morning," he told the men. "Anyone feel like making the trip?"

"Sure," Cussy said. "What am I getting?"

Dell avoided Calvin's curious stare. "I'll give you a list tomorrow. I've, uh, ordered some supplies."

Calvin kept staring. "What kind of supplies?"

"Just some things I think we need. Now, tell me about—"

"What kinds of things? Women things?"

Dell glared at him. "Things that you don't have to worry about, all right? Just some, uh, decorations to spruce the place up."

"I could use a new lamp," Rob said.

"Yeah," Jed agreed, grinning at his boss. "And a couple of them recliner chairs."

"We could plant some pretty flowers," Cussy suggested, winking at the others. "Since we have a lady visiting and all. Any idea how long she's staying, Dell?"

"No," he snapped. "We done here? Everyone knows what they're doing tomorrow?"

"Yeah," Cussy said, grinning. The others nodded. Calving was just about over, so everyone was perfectly willing to start putting in a normal day's work. Then Dell made sure he was back in the house by six-fifteen, in the shower by six-eighteen, and dressed for dinner at six twenty-nine. He remembered to shave and comb the damp hair off his forehead. He was no beauty, but at least he was clean.

6

"I HATE TO admit that this might be hopeless," Allison said, looking up at Dell with wide blue eyes. An Alan Jackson song blared in the background, and the babies were propped up on the couch where they could watch the dancing. For the moment they looked content, but Dell figured it was just a matter of time before they cried and he wouldn't have to dance anymore.

"I told you." He glanced over at them, just to make sure they didn't look upset, and then back down at his feet. He'd put on his dress boots for the dancing to-night, but fancy-dressed feet hadn't worked any better than the scruffy ones.

"Maybe it's the counting."

"Maybe," he agreed, looking down at her. She stood beside him, tiny and delicate in faded jeans and that white sweater that made her look like something from heaven. She'd pulled all that yellow hair into a knot at the nape of her neck, and her feet tapped in time to the music.

"One-two-three-four." Allison stepped in time to the music. "Step, step, side, heel. Now you do it."

Dell took a deep breath. He was determined to resist her, but it was pretty damn hard. He wanted to take her in his arms and waltz her around the room. If he could remember how to waltz, that is. He started to move.

"Say it out loud," Allison suggested. "With me."

"Step, step, side, heel." There. He'd done it. Would that please her? "You want to tell me why we're doing this?"

"So you can get out more and go dancing."

"You like to dance?"

"Sure. We—I used to go out once in a while. And they taught line dancing at my health club two nights a week. It was fun."

"I guess you'll go dancing in Seattle."

She chuckled. "I don't think so. I think those days are over." She smiled. "Sophie and Sylvie give me all the exercise I can handle." She looked down at his feet. "What about the two-step? Can you do that one?"

"I don't know." Two steps sounded better than learning combinations of eight or eighty kicks and slides. "I can try." There were a lot of things he could try, like making an excuse and going to bed early. He didn't have to torture himself by standing here breathing in the scent of Allison's hair. He was a grown man with a mind of his own; he could walk away.

Allison left his side to fiddle with the tape player. She walked back to him and stood in front of him. "Okay, here we go." She stepped closer and took his left hand, then put her tiny hand on his right shoulder. "It's one-two-*three*, one-two-*three*, fast-fast-*slow*, in time to the music. Don't worry about moving around too much. It'll come to you, if you listen to the beat."

He put his hand at her waist and wondered how he would be expected to listen to anything while he was holding her in his arms. He was paralyzed with fear and pleasure.

"Now," she said, trying to guide him. He didn't know how he managed to move, but he did. He'd danced at a couple of weddings, long ago, and the two-step was popular even then. He surprised himself by remembering when to move his feet.

"Wonderful," Allison murmured. "You're a natural."

He tripped. "Sorry. Guess you spoke too soon."

Her hand tightened in his. "No, you're doing fine." He managed to guide her around the part of the living room that didn't have furniture waiting to be bumped into. The babies stared at them as they passed the couch, and Allison called to them. "Hi, ladies! What do you think?"

Sylvie frowned, and Sophie's lips formed a little O. Dell stumbled, but recovered quickly. He tightened his hold on Allison's back and kept dancing until the song ended. He released her slowly. Too slowly, he figured, by the expression of surprise on her face.

"You all done?" Calvin called. They turned to see the older man standing in the doorway. He didn't look too happy. "I shoulda taken my hearing aid off before I came in here," he grumbled, rubbing his ear. "Ain't no saloon, you know."

Allison just smiled at him, turned off the tape player and turned to check on the girls. Sylvie sputtered, and Allison sat down on the couch and put the baby on her lap. "Hi, Cal. Would you like to join us?"

"Not me," the man replied, shaking his head. "I just came in to tell Dell something."

That figured, Dell thought. "What?"

"I'm going with Cuss in the mornin'." He took off his hat and sat down in the green recliner. "Thought I could use a trip to the big city."

"What city?" Allison adjusted her hold on the little girl, while her sister looked as if she couldn't decide if she wanted to be held, too. Dell walked over and picked up Sophie. He didn't want her to feel left out.

"Cheyenne," Cal supplied. "That music is gonna hurt the girlies' ears, if you ask me."

"It's not that loud." Dell shook his head. "Turn your hearing aid down."

Cal fiddled with his ear again. "I'm gonna get me another crock pot."

"Fine. Take the money out of the petty cash box."

"Already did." He eyed Allison. "You look like you got some rest. About time. Mothers have to take care of themselves."

"I did," she said, not looking too bothered by Cal's observations. "I mean, I am. Thanks to you."

"Me?"

"You took care of the babies again this morning so I could get on a horse."

"Wasn't nothin'," the older man muttered. "They were good as gold, the girlies were. I think they like our Wyoming air."

"I hope they sleep tonight," Allison said. "I'm trying to keep them awake this evening so they won't be awake half the night. I don't know what got into them last night."

"What d'ya mean?"

"They wanted to be held," she explained, shifting Sylvie's weight against her arm. "Look at her. She's happy now, but if I put her down she's probably going to cry."

"Oh." He studied the baby in Allison's arms, then turned to Dell. "Yours cry, too?"

"Not yet." Dell looked down at Sophie, whose blue-eyed gaze held his own. She was a sweet little thing, but both babies had minds of their own and weren't shy about letting everyone know what they wanted and when they wanted it. They were going to be a handful when they could talk. "When do babies start talking?"

"I'm not sure. I'll look it up in the baby book," Allison offered. "There's so much I don't know."

"You're doing fine," Dell assured her. He walked over to the couch and sat down at its far end. Sophie squawked, which meant she liked being held and walked better than being held on an old brown couch. He looked at his watch. It was after nine o'clock already. "You want help feeding them?"

"Well—"

Cal interrupted. "You done the payroll yet? The men expect their checks tomorrow, you know."

"I know." He'd started it early this morning, in the hour before the sun came up. "It's almost done."

"I'll feed them later. And I can do it by myself." Allison leaned back against the couch and studied the fieldstone fireplace. "I'll bet you have fires in the winter."

"Sometimes," Dell said, fighting the feeling of disappointment. He would have liked an excuse to be with Allison awhile longer. And he didn't mind feeding a baby or two, either. It was nice to have a little life in the house. He thought of tomorrow's delivery and hoped he'd done right. He'd tried to pick out the kinds of things a woman would like, the kinds of things that would make the old place look like someone cared.

Cal gave him a questioning look and Dell ignored him. He would do the payroll later, when he damn well felt like it.

"There's pineapple cake," his uncle said. "I guess I'm gonna cut myself a piece. Anyone else?" He hauled himself out of the recliner as Allison stood up, too, the baby still in her arms.

"I'll help," she offered.

He shrugged, and Dell could have kicked some sense into him. Just because the old cowboy was terrified of women, didn't mean that he had to be so damn obvious about it. "I will, too," Dell said, rising from the sofa with the baby in his arms. So the five of them ended up in the kitchen, and three of them ended up eating cake piled high with vanilla ice cream. It was the babies' cue to fuss, so Cal took Sophie so Allison could heat up the bottles. She took the babies, one at a time, into the bedroom to change their diapers, and then returned to the kitchen to feed them. Dell silently took Sophie and her bottle, while Cal looked on. If Dell didn't know better, he'd think his uncle was annoyed that he didn't have a baby to feed.

"I'm goin' to bed," the old man said, standing and putting his dirty dish in the sink. "Mornin' comes early, and Cuss wants to be on the road in good time. You want to give us a list or something, so we know what we're getting?"

No, he sure as hell didn't. "JCPenney has the order ready and waiting for you."

"Humph." Calvin shoved his hat onto his head and nodded to Allison. "'Night, ma'am."

"Good night, Calvin. Thanks again for watching the girls this morning."

"No problem."

He and Allison sat in silence for a few moments. The only noise was the suckling babies, until Allison stopped Sylvie at the halfway mark and lifted her to her shoulder to burp.

It was a strangely intimate situation, sitting at the

kitchen table with Allison. Sophie spit out her bottle and Dell imitated Allison's motion of putting the baby against his shoulder and patting her back with the gentlest of motions. The child burped delicately near Dell's ear, so he put her back in the cradle of his arms and tried to interest her in the rest of her bottle, but she pursed her little lips together and closed her eyes.

"I think she's done," he whispered as Allison continued to feed Sylvie. "And I think she's asleep."

"Okay," Allison said, keeping her voice low. "Can you wait a minute while I finish with Sylvie? Then I'll put them down and maybe they'll sleep for four or five hours tonight. I think we might have tired them out."

"Yeah." He looked down at the sleeping baby. "She looks like she won't wake up for a long while."

"I hope you're right." She chuckled, and Dell looked across the table into those beautiful blue eyes. "She can fool you."

"No," he said slowly. "I don't think so." He wasn't fooled at all. He knew animals, and he knew men. He didn't know women, but he'd bet his last section of prime grazing land that Allison was the woman who was meant for him. Up until now he hadn't thought there was anyone out there for him, or if there was, he wasn't going to meet her in Wells City. He'd wondered how it would happen, and he'd just about given up on it, too.

And here she was, sitting in his kitchen as if she'd always been here.

It damn well took his breath away.

Allison set the bottle on the table, burped the baby, and stood. "I'll be right back," she whispered.

"Is she asleep?"

"Just about. I'm going to try to put her down and see what happens."

He nodded and glanced down at the baby in his arms. Not much bigger than a football, but a thousand times prettier, of course. He carefully stood and the baby didn't wake at the movement, so he walked quietly down the hall toward the bedroom and peeked inside. Allison was bent over the babies' bed, tucking a blanket around the sleeping child. She straightened as Dell walked in and waited for him to bring the baby around to the side of the playpen.

"Should I do it?" he asked.

"Sure. If you don't mind."

He shook his head. "No." He bent over and lay the child near her sister, then moved to the side while Allison fussed with the blankets. She touched his arm when she was finished.

"Thank you for helping," she said. "It's been really hard these past months by myself."

"No problem," he managed to say. She was looking up at him as if he'd given her bags of diamonds. "Glad to help."

She continued to look up at him with those blue eyes. "You would have liked my sister. She would have been a good mother, if she'd gotten the chance."

"You're doing okay," he assured her. And then, he didn't know why, Allison raised on her tiptoes and kissed him on the cheek.

"Thank you," she said. "You're a good man, Wendell Jones."

His face burned where her lips had touched him and before she moved away Dell tilted his head and met her lips with his own. He didn't know why. It just seemed natural to kiss that warm-skinned woman in the dim light of a room that smelled of baby powder.

She tasted of sugar and ice cream, and her lips were soft and surprisingly responsive under his. He wanted to stand there and kiss her for hours, but instead Dell lifted his mouth from hers after only a few brief seconds. He looked down at her, tried to form the words to apologize, and failed. She didn't say anything, either, so he spun on his heel and left the room as fast as he could without running.

Later, in the privacy of his bedroom, he stared out the window toward the main road. There was nothing to see, of course. There never was. But his own reflection shone back and Dell knew he was looking at the biggest fool who ever called Wyoming home.

OKAY, SHE SHOULDN'T have kissed him. She'd always been told she was too warmhearted, too impulsive, too much of a risk-taker. But she'd sincerely meant to thank him. She'd been overcome with such gratitude for his quiet strength, for his kindness to her and the children. So she'd reached up and kissed his cheek. And then that's when it happened. His dark eyes had widened just the smallest bit, and he'd turned his head just an inch or so, and he'd kissed her. On the lips. Briefly.

Allison closed her eyes again and pulled the covers up to her chin. She'd gone to bed right after the babies, right after Dell had left her. She hadn't bothered to try to read, though the small light from the reading lamp didn't bother the girls. She was only thirty pages or so into that serial killer mystery and it was already scaring her.

And now other things were scaring her, like being

attracted to the big rancher. And feeling something when his lips had touched hers. She didn't want to feel anything for anyone. Except the children. Her parents had died; they'd had no business being in that sailboat race on Lake Michigan, but they'd gone anyway. Despite Dad's bad heart and the fact that Mother couldn't swim. And then it had just been Sandy and Allison, for the past three years. Until Sandy was hit by a drunk driver. They'd kept her alive long enough to deliver the babies, and then she was gone.

Allison wiped the tears that dripped silently down her face and turned onto her side, away from the sleeping children. Tomorrow she would find out about her car, she would pin down that enigmatic mechanic and make him tell her when her car would be fixed, and then she would make plans to leave the Lazy J.

It would be for the best.

"WHERE THE HELL do you want all this stuff?"

"Here's fine," Dell answered, and then the rest of his words were muffled by the cursing of another man and the sound of a door banging shut.

Allison, a baby in each arm, couldn't help wondering what was going on in the living room. She came out of the kitchen and peered into the room just as Calvin set down a big cardboard box. Allison watched from the safety of the kitchen as the three men brought in packages and boxes, set them down in the middle of the room and then looked at Dell for an explanation.

"What the hell is this?" Cal handed his nephew a piece of paper as Cussy hurried out the front door. "Here's your receipt. Just a lot of numbers on it, though. Didn't say what anything was."

Dell glanced at the list and tossed it on the couch.

"I'm fixing up the house." He waved his arms toward the bare walls. "Thought it was about time."

"Humph," was all Calvin replied. "What for?"

"It looks pretty damn bad, that's why." Dell's gaze met Allison's and he flushed and looked away.

"Well, it's your house," Cal sighed, scratching the back of his neck. "You can do what you want, but I kinda liked this room the way it was. 'Course when your ma was alive I guess it looked better."

"Hard to remember," Dell muttered. "Dad packed up most of the stuff."

"I hope you're not making a big mistake, son." He turned and saw Allison in the doorway, but he didn't smile. He stared at her and the babies in her arms, and then he sighed. "You need some help with the girlies?"

"No, I've got—"

But he took Sylvie out of her arms and held her as if he'd been holding babies all his life. Dell didn't move, but he nodded briefly to acknowledge her presence at the edge of the room.

Allison stood there, feeling awkward. They'd avoided each other all day, or at least that is what Allison figured they were doing. Successfully, too. The house had been empty and quiet when she fed the babies their late morning bottle. They'd woken at four, taken their bottles, and gone back to sleep until nine. So had Allison. The only evidence that Dell had been in the house was the coffee mug in the sink.

"Aren't you gonna start opening these?"

Dell tore his gaze away from Allison. "Yeah, sure. In a while."

"Why not now?" his uncle asked, moving closer to the largest box. "You're making me and the girlie here pretty damn curious."

"Well," Dell drawled, tapping the top of the box with long fingers, "I guess I could do that now."

Allison stepped closer to see. It looked like Christmas in the living room and she couldn't imagine what kinds of things a Wyoming rancher would order in Cheyenne. A new television, perhaps? Or some saddles or blankets? Maybe the boxes were packed with blue jeans and work shirts for all of the men for the summer. Dell pulled a jackknife from his pocket and began to open the top of the largest box. He slit open one side, then managed to pull out a wide rocking chair.

"That'll come in handy," Calvin drawled. "If you're planning on havin' babies."

"We have babies now," Dell muttered.

Allison peered over the cardboard flaps. The sturdy rocker was a light oak and quite pretty. Flowered blue cushions lined the back and seat. "I hope you didn't buy it just for the girls."

"You needed one," was all the cowboy said. "A big one."

She thought it was time to point out that she and the girls would be leaving soon. She hadn't figured out how to accomplish this yet, especially not after calling the Wells City mechanic this morning. The man had not been very optimistic about receiving a replacement axle anytime soon.

"I talked to the mechanic today," she began.

Dell looked up. "And?"

"He made it sound like the search for the Holy Grail."

"I'm sure he'll find something eventually," Dell said, turning to another box. He started slicing open the top flaps.

"So I've been thinking," she said, watching him remove a pale pink—*pink?*—chest of drawers from the box. "I think I'll rent a car and keep going."

"What about the Probe?" He set the chest against the bare wall by the door, then began opening another box.

"I'll sell it."

"This is ranch country, Allison. People around here aren't in the market for a car like that." This time the cardboard opening revealed a fancy gold-painted mirror. "What do you think?" He held it up.

Allison saw a tired-looking woman with limp hair and a sleeping baby in her arms. "It's very nice. Where are you going to put it?"

"Your room," he said. "I think that part of the house needs sprucing up, don't you?"

"Well—"

"You're a decorator, right? Wouldn't you say the place needs some spark?"

She gulped. The rocker was acceptable, but the pink dresser and the gold-edged mirror were two things that looked more out of place at the ranch than she did. "I think your house is very nice."

"It's bare," Dell declared. Calvin, looking like he was enjoying himself, sat down on the couch and cradled the baby in his arms.

Allison searched for something to say, something that would make him realize that pink and gold were not right for the ranch. The room was a large one, but the walls needed a fresh coat of soft ivory paint, the stone hearth needed scrubbing and if the couch was moved and that coffee table tossed out... "What about a nice new rug?"

"I thought of that. Got a braided one, like my mother used to have in this room."

"Good."

"Hard to decide between that and an Oriental one, though. I could use some help, I guess," he said. "If you weren't determined to leave, you could—well, never mind."

"I could help you...arrange things," she said, approaching the rocking chair.

"Try it, see if it works," he said.

She did, and it did. "After all, that's what I do—what I used to do—for a living."

"Did you like that kind of job?"

"Sure. Although it's less glamorous than it sounds." She didn't say that her boyfriend had been her partner, or that she'd spent endless hours working on the business only to have to walk away from it. The funny thing was, she hadn't missed working. Maybe, she thought wryly, looking down at the baby in her arms, she hadn't had time to miss much of anything. At least the babies kept her from having the time and energy to think. "Do you have chairs for the dining room table?"

"Yeah. Out in the shed."

"What do they look like?"

"Well..." He looked confused. "Like the table, I guess. Kind of dark and plain."

"Your couch is in good shape, and so are the recliners. A few pillows would brighten things up, and maybe some bookcases, too. In oak, to match the rest of the furniture."

"You want to look at the catalog?"

"Sure." He bent down to his stack of magazines and pulled out a thick JCPenney catalogue.

"Just put it on the couch for now. I'll go through it later. I guess Wells City doesn't have any furniture stores."

"No, ma'am."

"Do you, um, have a budget for this project?"

Cal chuckled. "He don't like to spend money, Allison."

Dell, a fierce expression on his face, glared at his uncle in a way that made Allison want to laugh. If she didn't know him, she might be afraid, but she knew that underneath that giant body beat a giant heart.

"It looks like he spent some today," she said, looking around the room. "What's in the other boxes?"

"Lamps. Some wicker chairs for the porch. I thought we'd fix up the front porch while we're at it. Anything you don't like, I mean, that you don't think is right, can go back."

"All right." That was a relief. She smiled at him and stood. "Let me put the girls down for their nap, and then we'll talk about finding those dining room chairs."

"We never use the table," Cal muttered.

"But it would look nice," she noted. "And the room is large enough to hold much more than it does. It might make it look homier."

"Homey," Dell repeated, looking almost happy. "That's exactly what I had in mind."

"Good," said Allison, pleased that she could finally do something to repay his hospitality. "I'll get some paper and start making a list while you find the dining room chairs. And do you have a tape measure?"

"I'll find one," Dell promised, and Allison couldn't help but smile at him. The kiss last night had been a silly mistake, an accident in the darkness, and she knew it would never happen again.

"HOMEY," Cal muttered, crossing the muddy yard. He said the word as if it was an evil adjective out to destroy the ranch. He spit in the dirt and kept moving toward the bunkhouse. "Homey, my ass."

"What are you mutterin' about?" Rob called from the porch. "Your face is gonna set in stone like that and you'll scare the girlies."

"Damn fool nephew of mine bought himself some new furniture."

The cowboy's expression brightened. "That mean we get the old stuff?"

Calvin shrugged, and pushed the door open. He sat down in the empty chair, stretched his legs out in front of him and adjusted his hearing aid. It had been a long drive to town, but he and Cussy had eaten their fill of chicken-fried steak at that big diner outside of Cheyenne. That, and the mashed potatoes, had been worth the trip. "He's 'decoratin'.' And Miss Allison is helping him."

"Well, that's nice. They'd make a right nice couple."

The older man snorted. "She's a beauty, all right, and he's, well, he's a good man—"

"Finer man never lived," Rob agreed solemnly.

"But he's not much for looks, and he doesn't know nothing about women and he's going to get his heart broken."

Rob frowned. "I heard in town that she was, well, his girlfriend."

"She ain't. And that's the problem."

"She leavin?"

"Yep. When that silly car of hers gets fixed."

"The boss is sure nicer these days."

"You wait," Cal said ominously. "When she leaves, there'll be hell to pay around here. He'll be like a grizzly with a bullet in his thigh, and there won't be no pleasin' him. She's gonna decorate his house and break his heart and there's not a damn thing anyone can do about it."

"You could," the younger man said. "He listens to you about lots of things."

"Not about women," he muttered. "Not about *this* woman he's not listening."

"Maybe she'll stay. Become the missus. Then the boss would be in a good mood all the time."

Cal shook his head. "Nope. I got a bad feelin'." The other cowboy was silent. Cal's bad feelings were legendary, and to be respected. "I gotta do some thinkin'," the old man declared. "Before all hell breaks loose."

7

"Is THIS WHERE you want it?" Dell tried to hide his
smile of satisfaction. This was working out better than
he thought. Allison had been busy with the living
room for two days. Thankfully she'd been too busy to
mind that her car was still in Wells City, too busy to
blush when she caught him looking at her and he knew
she was remembering that brief kiss just the way he
was.

"Over here. I think," Allison ordered, pointing to an
empty place in front of her. Dell and Rob picked up the
couch and moved it to where she directed, then
watched her frown. Her gaze darted around the room
as if she was redoing the whole floor plan in her head.
Every now and then she'd study the paper she held in
her hand.

She pointed to the recliners. "Would you put one to
the left and one to the right of the fireplace?" She
sighed. "This is a big room, but those recliners are giving me fits. I should put one in the corner with a reading light and a bookcase."

He didn't offer to take them out of the room. No way
was he going through football season without his reclining chair, and Cal would feel the same way. And
the chairs were only a few years old, so they had some
living left to do, that was for sure. Not even for Allison
would he give up his chair. She'd moved the stacks of

books and magazines out to the porch and, over his protests, she'd scrubbed the wooden floor until it gleamed, and taken the old curtains down from the windows. The place looked better already.

"I don't know," she muttered. She bent over and patted the brown cushions into place, which gave him a heart-stopping view of that cute little bottom of hers. Those faded jeans fit her real well, and Dell considered moving his recliner out to the bunkhouse. There was good reception out there as well.

"I could—"

"No," she said, shaking her head. "We're not moving it again. This is the only spot that takes advantage of the fireplace." The younger cowhand rolled his eyes in relief, but Allison didn't notice. She turned to Dell. "You said you have a fire in the winter, right?"

"Yep." He would build one tonight, just to prove it. He would show her that the room could be warm and comfortable, especially if the lights were off.

"All right, then." She waved toward the rocker and the men backed away from the couch.

"You can go," Dell told the young man. "There's nothing else I can't handle." Besides, he'd seen Rob blush whenever Allison had smiled at him. There was no sense torturing the kid any longer. "Tell Cussy to come get me if he needs me for anything."

"Sure, boss." The cowboy grabbed his hat. "Goodbye, ma'am. You just holler if you need me."

"Thank you." Allison flashed another one of those angelic smiles and the cowboy flushed pink to the tips of his ears before he realized he was supposed to be leaving, not standing beside his boss and grinning like the village idiot.

"I appreciate your doing this," Dell said once again.

"It's the least I can do to earn my keep around here," she answered, giving him another one of those quick smiles before turning back to the chart in her hand. "I wish I had time to paint the walls."

"I can paint."

"Really?"

"Of course. I'm willing to do whatever it takes."

"Why?"

"What?"

"Why are you going to all this trouble now?" she asked. "Usually people redecorate for a reason, like a party or expecting company or for someone new in the—" She stopped and stared up at him. "Are you expecting a life-style change?"

"A what?"

"I knew you were just teasing when you said you didn't date."

He didn't know what in hell she was talking about. "I don't."

"Then why are you fixing the place up?"

Dell felt like a cornered bear. He drew himself up to his full height and frowned at the tiny woman in front of him. He'd be damned if he was ready to explain that he hoped she and the babies would stay. He wasn't even sure he was ready to admit it to himself more than once a day, but he was going ahead with the decorating bullshit just in case. The old house needed a good sprucing up, whether he slept alone or not. "Seemed like a good idea," was all he could manage through gritted teeth.

Those blue eyes didn't waver. "Hmm," was all she said, then turned back to her chart. "You wanted the front porch fixed up, too?"

"If it's not too much trouble."

"No, I think that's a great idea. Paint will do wonders for both rooms."

"I'll send one of the men to town. What color do you want?"

She turned to him again. "You have to pick out the color."

He shrugged. "White's fine."

"No, there are too many different kinds. You have to pick."

"No," he countered, putting his hands on his hips. "You're the decorator. *You* have to pick." That made her eyes twinkle and, as a result, he felt his heart beat faster. It seemed to do that a lot lately.

"Okay. Can I borrow a truck?"

"I'll take you myself."

"Are you worried that I'll end up in another ditch?" she teased.

"That's possible. You don't know the roads." He backed up a couple of steps. "You want to go now? I'll see if Cal will watch the girls."

Allison hesitated, but she was clearly interested in buying paint. "You don't think he'd mind? They just went to sleep ten minutes ago, so they should be napping for at least a couple of hours. It won't take me long to pick out paint."

"Hell, Cal won't mind. He's pleased that I'm finally getting around to fixing up this place," Dell lied. "He'll be glad to help."

"He didn't look too happy last night, when we moved his chair."

"I think he likes the rocker better anyway," Dell said.

"We can stop at the station and check on the car,"

Allison said, picking up a pen. "And I'd better buy some more formula. I'll make a list."

Dell looked around the room and wondered if he would get used to the changes. Was he being foolish hoping he could entice her to stay here on the ranch? Or was he smart enough to know not to let Allison walk out of his life without a fight? Only time would tell, and his time was running out.

"NOVEMBER," Allison announced, tapping the card with the selection of ivory shades striping its surface. "I think that's the best one. Don't you?" She didn't want to push her choice on him, of course, because she didn't believe in bullying clients to accept her taste. On the other hand, she worked hard to ensure the finished projects would be special.

Dell didn't so much as glance at the card. "Sure," he drawled, his gaze dropping to the bin of paintbrushes by his knees. "Get whatever you want."

"I want you to be happy with it," she said, holding up the card in the vicinity of his chin. "You're the one who has to live with it."

"Allison." He gently pushed the card aside and looked down at her with the patient expression she'd seen him use with the younger cowhands. "You're the decorator. I'm the rancher."

"Well..." She hesitated. *Snowflake* would be a good color, too. And she wanted it to be perfect for Dell; she wanted to leave him with a comfortable and pleasant living room that would make him feel good at the end of every long day. She studied the card once again, tilting it to get the best light. "We'll go with *November* then."

Dell waved over the clerk. "Joe? We need ten gallons of something called November."

"Indoor satin latex," Allison added. The man nodded, took the card from Allison and disappeared into the back room. Within ten minutes the paint, mixed and shaken, was stored in the back of Dell's truck, the bag with the brushes, rollers and pads tucked between the cans of paint and a case of baby formula.

"Could we stop and check on my car?"

He hesitated, or at least she thought he did. "Sure," he said, guiding the truck through town. He pulled up across the street and offered to go inside and talk to Pete himself. "If you don't mind?" he added.

Allison was only too glad to let a man handle it. She rolled down the window and took a deep breath of fresh spring air. She still needed to wear a jacket, and her long flannel nightgown felt cozy at night, but there was no doubt that spring was coming, and coming soon. Even to Wyoming. She watched the people going in and out of the diner and wondered who they were, if they lived in town or were ranchers who had come to town to do their errands. They looked as if they were glad that winter was over, too.

Dell came out of the gas station and strode across the street toward her side of the truck. "Come on," he said, opening her door. "I'll buy you a malt." When she hesitated, he added, "Cal and the girlies will be fine."

She stepped out of the truck and the wind whipped her hair around her face. "I saw a used furniture store on the side street by the post office. I thought we could stop and look around before we went home."

"I've got a shed full of that stuff," he muttered, ushering her into the warmth of the diner. "My father never threw anything away, and I guess I'm just like him."

"What did the mechanic say about my car?"

He didn't look at her. "It's going to be a while. No one has the part, and it's looking like it will be faster to take out your axle and rebuild it. If you don't mind."

She hurried to keep up with him. "Did he say how much it would cost?"

"Between four hundred and six hundred dollars." He gave her a sympathetic glance as he opened the door to the diner. "You're to call him when you decide."

Allison's heart sank. That was a lot of money, but she really had no choice. She couldn't stay in Wyoming forever.

"Hey, Dell!"

"Hey, Lucille," Dell said, touching the small of Allison's back and directing her toward a booth by the window. Allison gave the redheaded waitress her best smile and watched as the woman pretended not to notice her again. The waitress followed them, tossed two plastic-coated menus on the table and smiled at Dell once again. She even went so far as to lay her hand on Dell's wide shoulder.

"I see you still have company," she said, nodding to Allison.

"Yep," she said. "I'm still here."

"How long are you going to stay? Dell hasn't scared you out of town yet?"

Allison looked at Dell and touched his arm. "I don't know. Dell, how long am I staying?"

Dell cleared his throat and ignored the question. "I think we're going to have malts. Chocolate or vanilla, Allison?"

"Vanilla, please."

"Chocolate for me, Lucille." Dell handed her the menus and she took her hand from his shoulder.

"That's all? No fries?"

"No. Cal's making enchiladas tonight. I don't want to spoil my appetite."

"A big lug like you shouldn't worry about appetites." Lucille tucked her order pad into the pocket of her pink apron. "Tell the old buzzard that we put him down to bake rolls for the May Day fund-raiser. He'll want to buy raffle tickets, too."

"I'll tell him."

She returned to the counter and gave the order to another woman behind the counter.

"That woman brings out the worst in me," Allison muttered.

"I noticed."

"I don't like the way she looks at you." Dell raised his bushy eyebrows. "Like she's making fun."

"It's just her way, Allison."

"She can keep 'her way' to herself," she muttered, feeling a little ridiculous about the stab of jealousy she'd felt when Lucille touched Dell. There was no reason to feel that way. It wasn't as if she was involved with the big rancher. He most likely had a girlfriend here in the county somewhere, no matter what he said to the contrary. "Please tell me she isn't your girlfriend."

He looked at her and then burst out laughing. "That's the truth."

"Well, then, who is?"

"Who is what?"

"You're fixing up your house, Dell. There must be an ulterior motive."

Guilt flashed across his face for just a second, then he frowned at her. It was a fierce expression, but she knew better than to believe he was really angry. "Don't look at me like that," she said.

"Like what?"

"Like you're going to act like an old dog and start growling at me. I simply asked you a question."

Lucille plopped two empty glasses, two large metal containers and two straws in front of them. "Enjoy," she said. "Now that you're a man-about-town, Dell, you should give me a call sometime, when you're free."

"Thanks," he said, ignoring the invitation. Or maybe, Allison thought, noticing the way he concentrated on pouring the malts into the glasses, he didn't understand that the waitress was inviting him to do more than call her on the telephone. Unless she was teasing again, in which case Allison figured the woman had a mean streak longer than her fingernails.

"Does she give you a hard time every time you come in here?"

"No." He looked surprised. "Is that what she was doing?"

Allison stuck her straw in the drink and took a sip before she answered. She didn't understand why Lucille irritated her so much, except that she knew the waitress was not the right woman for Wendell Jones. "That's exactly what she was doing. And she was flirting with you, too. Do you really think she'd make a good ranch wife?"

"Lucille just teases, that's all. She's been calling me names and giving me a hard time since we were in fourth grade."

Allison didn't like it one bit. The kind rancher didn't

deserve to be laughed at. "I don't think that's very nice."

He shrugged. "Honey, when you're as big and ugly as I am, you get used to it. The Joneses aren't known for their great beauty," he added, chuckling.

"You're not ugly." Allison looked into his handsome brown eyes and wondered how anyone could tease such a kind man. There wasn't a mean or vicious bone in his body. He was probably just *too* nice for his own good. "You're the strong, rugged cowboy type of man, that's all."

"You've been watching too many John Wayne movies."

"That's a perfect example. John Wayne. He was a big man, and not exactly the best-looking man in the world, either. But he was rough and tough and had a certain presence. People respected him." She took a sip of the malt and looked past Dell's shoulder toward the counter. Lucille and two older men were joking and laughing and looking in Dell's direction. She didn't know why it amused them all so much to see Dell sitting in the diner drinking a malt with a friend, but if they were so hard up for conversation, she intended to give them something to talk about.

Dell shook his head. "You sure get some strange notions. I'm no movie—"

"Kiss me," she said, leaning forward.

Dell stared at her. "What?"

She moved her glass out of the way and leaned farther across the table. "Kiss me. Right here. Right now."

"Hell, no."

"Please?" She glanced toward the counter again to see that they were still the topic of amusement, then moved Dell's glass out of the way.

"When I make love to a woman, I like to do it in private." He reached for his glass, but Allison stopped him by touching his forearm.

"Dammit, Dell. Just do it." She tugged him forward, and he leaned toward her, a questioning expression on his big square face. "Pretend you want me," she whispered.

She leaned forward as much as she dared, until Dell closed the gap between them, cupped one large hand behind the nape of her neck and touched his lips to hers. He tilted his head, slanting his mouth across hers in a heart-stopping motion. Allison felt that surprising jolt of passion again, wondered where on earth it came from, closed her eyes and stopped thinking. He tasted of chocolate and his lips, cool against hers, sent lovely shivers down the back of her neck. Allison forgot where they were for the long moments of the kiss, until Dell released her. He leaned back against the red vinyl seat, picked up his glass and took a long swallow of chocolate malt. All Allison could do was stare at him. She tingled right down to her toes and in other parts of her anatomy that she didn't want to think about right now. She couldn't remember the last time she'd been so affected by a kiss.

The café was silent. So silent that Allison wondered if she'd gone deaf. She forgot to look at Lucille. Instead she watched Dell take a paper napkin from the holder bolted to the wall and wipe chocolate milk from his upper lip. He pulled out his wallet, selected a five dollar bill and tossed it on the table.

"We'd better get going. Are you ready?" he asked.

She nodded. Her hearing had returned, but would her legs hold her up once she'd slid out of the booth? Dell stood, waited for Allison to join him, then called his thanks to Lucille. The expression on his face was impassive, and his tone friendly and casual. Allison gazed at him, but he didn't look at her. How could he be so calm after such a kiss? Maybe kissing was different for men. Or different for men in Wyoming. Or different—

"Allison?" Dell held the door open for her and waited for her to go through it.

He followed her outside, walking to the truck and opening her door. Allison climbed in, watched as he shut the door and strolled around to the other side of the truck. He turned on the ignition, made a U-turn in the middle of the empty street, and headed back to the ranch. Allison waited for him to say something, anything, but he didn't. He fiddled with the radio until a country-western station came in clear enough to whistle to while she looked out the window at the brown, rolling hills. There were barbed-wire fences and the occasional cow, dirt roads heading off from the highway, and once Allison thought she saw an antelope. She thought of asking Dell if that's what it was, but thought better of it.

She didn't really feel like talking. She needed to think over what had happened this afternoon. As if she didn't have enough to worry about, now she had to decide what to do with her puzzling physical attraction to a stranger. There was no denying the attraction, at least on her part. Those intimate parts of her body were reminding her that she had found that kiss very, very exciting. And unfulfilling. Her body clamored for more, and her heart knew better than to entertain the idea.

Dell turned onto the private road that led to the Lazy J. He slowed down after he'd rounded the first turn and stopped the truck before climbing the hill that led to the ranch house. After he switched off the ignition he turned to Allison.

"Come here," was all he said in that same expressionless voice.

Allison gulped. "Why?"

"Just do it," he said, mimicking her words in the diner.

She inched closer to him, until her hip hit the gearshift's black knob. He put his hands on her upper arms and lifted her onto his lap. Then he kissed her, but this time there was no hesitation in the motion. His lips were warm and demanding, and when he urged her lips apart Allison didn't think to protest the intimacy. His chest was like an iron wall against her breasts, and Dell held her arms so she couldn't move, couldn't wrap her arms around him the way she wanted to. He made love to her mouth for long, body-melting moments, until Allison whimpered with need and desire. He released her then, and lifted her back onto her seat.

Allison took a deep breath. "What was that for?" she asked, embarrassed to hear the way her voice shook.

"I told you," he replied, not sounding too calm himself. "When I make love to a woman, I like to do it in private."

"You're angry about the diner. I'm sorry."

He gave her a look she could only describe as furious, then turned away from her. He gripped the steering wheel until his big knuckles turned white. "I don't like being played for a fool," he told the windshield.

"That's not—"

"And I don't like games."

"I wasn't—"

"And don't ever put your arms around me again and tell me to pretend." He started up the truck and headed home. Allison sat in miserable silence. She would call Mayme to come get her. She would take the babies and go home. She didn't know what else to do, because falling in love with Wendell Jones was something that made absolutely no sense at all.

"THE LITTLE GAL is packing up," Calvin informed his nephew. "You got any idea what's going on?"

"She can't go anywhere," he muttered. He sat on a bale of hay in a corner of the barn and put his head in his hands.

"Is her car fixed? I didn't see it out in the front yard." He tried not to sound as hopeful as he felt.

"No, and it won't be for a while longer." He sighed. "I paid Pete to stall on the repairs to that car of hers. He couldn't find an axle, but he promised to take his time rebuilding hers." He would have to apologize. He knew that, and dreaded it.

Cal was silent as he digested that bit of information. He sat down on the bale of hay beside Dell. "Why is Allison in such an all-fired hurry to get out of here then? She's on the phone gettin' a bus schedule right now."

Dell didn't answer. He wasn't about to explain this afternoon to his uncle. He wasn't sure how he could explain it anyway.

"She can't get on a bus with those babies," Cal continued. "Ain't right. One of the boys could take her into Cheyenne, I guess. But that don't seem like the right thing, either."

No, Allison and the babies all alone again wasn't right at all. They needed a home. Allison didn't need a horny cowboy groping her in his pickup truck. "I should be shot."

"Well, son, I don't think it could be that bad," Cal drawled. "Women are tricky creatures. They get upset and then they get over it in a little while with a little sweet talk."

"No offense, Cal, but how did you get to be such an expert?"

"I've had some experience. When I was in the navy. And before that, too," Cal added, sounding injured. "Hell, son, I'm sixty-five years old and I've sweet-talked a few women in my younger days."

"I'm not much for sweet talking." He winced, thinking of how he'd grabbed her and put her on his lap. She could have bruised from the steering wheel.

"Well, that's true. I thought you were gonna practice with Allison."

He'd practiced a lot more than talking, Dell thought. He'd kissed her twice in less than twenty-four hours. He'd had to grip the steering wheel of the truck in order not to take her in his arms and do it again. "Well, that didn't work out in the way I thought it would."

"Humph."

Dell sat up and eyed his uncle. "I guess I'd better go apologize."

"You?"

"First time for everything," he stated, rising to his feet. "Guess I'd better get to it." He shoved his hands into his pockets and gazed toward the barn door, but he didn't move.

Calvin struggled to his feet and put his hand on the younger man's arm. "You ain't in love, are you, Dell?"

"In love? I don't know." He shrugged. "I think I'm out of my goddam mind." He adjusted his hat and squared his shoulders. "Guess I'd better get to it." He strode out of the barn and into the bright sunlight.

"Supper's gonna be ready in forty minutes," Cal hollered. "You can take it out of the oven yourself."

Dell lifted his hand to show he'd heard him, but he didn't turn around. He had forty minutes to talk Allison into staying. He had forty minutes to redeem himself for acting like a fool so she'd eat supper with him. He wasn't sorry he'd kissed her, though. He was just sorry about the way he'd done it. In anger and frustration.

He was sure going to hate eating alone again. How did you tell a woman that wanting her so much made a man do foolish things?

SHE WASN'T EVEN CLOSE to falling in love with Dell Jones, she reminded herself as she pulled the babies' clean clothes from the dryer and folded them. She wasn't close to falling in love with anyone. She stacked tiny pink sleepers next to the stack of blankets on top of the dryer until there was nothing left to fold.

Therefore, Allison decided, she was in no position to kiss anyone. She had no intention of falling in love again, ever. Except maybe after the girls were grown and life calmed down enough to contemplate marriage. Maybe by that time, in eighteen or twenty years, she'd feel confident enough to make a commitment, to make the right decision.

God knows, her track record making decisions wasn't going to win any awards. Moving to Kansas City, her partnership with Ryan, the resulting engagement and living together; all were examples of bad decisions. She'd hoped to clean the slate with the move to Seattle. Starting over, the three of them, leaving the baggage behind them in the rearview mirror. She watched out the window as Dell crossed the yard between the barn and the house. His hat shaded his face, but she could tell he wasn't happy. He would be happy when she told him she was leaving. He would be glad to see the last of her, of that she was sure.

He came in the back door and took three steps into the storage room before he realized she was standing there.

He cleared his throat and removed his hat. "Cal said you're packing up to leave."

"Maybe that would be for the best."

Dell's steady gaze didn't waver as he looked down at her. "Maybe, maybe not."

Allison took a deep breath and let it out. "You're angry about this afternoon, and I don't blame you. It was terribly wrong of me to embarrass you in front of your...friends."

"I was angry," he admitted, twisting the brim of his hat. "I thought...well, never mind."

"I'm sorry." Truer words had never been spoken. She piled the babies' clothes in her arms and turned back to the rancher. "It will never happen again. I've called a bus company. If someone could give me a ride to Wells City in the morning, the girls and I can be on the eight-ten bus to Cheyenne."

"And then what?"

"We wait. From a motel. Where we can't bother anyone."

He frowned and looked fierce, but Allison was used to that expression. "You're not bothering anyone here."

"I can't stay here," she said. "We're in the way."

"I, uh, had another idea," he said, his voice low. He looked at her and frowned again. "I want to hire you. Officially."

"To do what?"

"Fix up the house. The porch, the bedroom—yours, I mean, not mine—and the men's bunkhouse. It's about time it got a fresh coat of paint."

"You don't have to *hire* me for that. I was happy to help."

"But you're leaving before the job is finished," he stated flatly, much to her embarrassment. "I'd kinda like to see what the living room would look like with a little paint and some new pillows." He jammed his hat back onto his head as if he were afraid he'd tear it to shreds otherwise. "You did say you would order pillows?"

"Yes. A nice plaid with green and br—"

"Allison."

She stopped and pressed her lips together.

"What happened today will never happen again. You have my word."

Oh, why did her heart fall to her knees with that promise? "It won't?"

"No."

"I'm not going to take your money," she said. "I'm glad I can do something to help you."

"You'll stay."

It wasn't a question, but she nodded her assent. "I'll think about it." She gripped the clothes tighter against her chest and moved toward the kitchen. "I'd better go put these away. The girls are awake, but I don't think they'll be happy playing in their bed for much longer."

"Cal made out all right?" He followed her through the kitchen and down the hall toward the distant bedroom.

"Just fine. He has such a knack with them."

"Yeah, I've noticed."

Allison paused by the babies' bed and peeked at the girls, who looked up at her with big blue eyes. "Hello, sweethearts. Did you miss me?"

Sylvie smiled and Sophie blew a bubble from her lips. Dell leaned over the bed. "Can I pick them up?"

"Sure." She put the clothes on the bed and waited a few seconds before she turned back to the cowboy who'd promised he would never kiss her again. She turned and watched the careful way he lifted Sophie into his arms.

"Hey, there," he said, not looking fierce at all. "You want your supper, too?" Sophie gurgled her answer.

Allison didn't know why she should feel as if she'd lost something special.

8

"THE BOSS was hidin' in the barn this afternoon," Cussy announced to the other men at the table. "Hidin' like a goddam fugitive, sadder than hell. Never thought I'd live to see the day when a woman brought down a giant like Wendell Jones. In my day a man had better sense than to skulk around a barn feeling sorry for himself."

"How do you know?" Jed asked. "You want to hand that salt down here?"

Cussy slid the salt shaker down the length of the plastic-coated table. "Saw him myself. Ain't that right, Cal?"

Calvin sighed, helped himself to two more enchiladas and debated whether or not to talk to the men about this latest development in the Ranch Romance, as he was starting to think of it. When he could bear thinking about it, that was. He looked up from his meal to see all seven men looking at him and waiting for an answer. "He's in there apologizing to her."

The older men gasped, though the younger ones didn't seem concerned with that particular piece of information.

"No kidding," Cussy said, clearly shocked. "I never heard the boss apologize."

"Well, you ain't never seen him around a little yellow-haired woman, either."

"True," the man admitted. "Guess that would make a difference, all right."

"Women can do that," someone else insisted. "Make a man crazy, don't they?"

They ate in silence while Calvin pondered his nephew's future. He didn't think it looked too bright. Even if Allison forgave him—for what he couldn't even begin to imagine—that still left Dell in pretty bad shape. His poor nephew was in love, and that woman wasn't the one to make him happy either. She was trouble, all right, from the first time he'd seen her Cal had known that nothin' good could come from her arrival on the Lazy J.

"Is Dell going to be all right?"

Calvin shrugged. "He's in love."

"No way," someone said, scraping back his chair. He went to the sink and refilled his water glass. "Dammit, Cal, that salsa's hot!"

"I didn't make you pour it all over your meal," Calvin pointed out, spearing another forkful.

"She's a nice little gal. Real friendly."

"And I like holding those girlies. What are you gonna do with all the money you're making, Cal?"

He shrugged. "Haven't decided," he lied. He figured he was entitled to his secrets. He adjusted his hearing aid as the clatter of dishes started to hurt his ear.

"I'll bet Dell marries her," a young cowboy said, sounding sad.

Cussy leaned forward. "How much?"

"Five dollars."

"That's all? Chicken feed."

"Hardly worth the effort to bet," someone else added.

"All right," the young man said, sticking out his chin. "Fifty." He dared the older man to take his bet. "I'll bet fifty bucks that Dell marries her. I know I would if I was in his boots."

"Humph," was all Calvin could say. He didn't hold much with gambling, but that didn't mean he wasn't up for a little friendly bet once in a while. "You're on," he said.

"I'm in," Cussy added. "Fifty bucks says Dell stays a bachelor."

The other men divided up evenly, and Calvin consented to hold the money. "You men have a time limit on this?"

Cussy rolled his eyes heavenward, as if to ask the Lord's opinion. "By the first of June," he said. "A man ought to be able to hog-tie a woman within a month, right?"

There was no answer to that question, as none of the men in the room had successfully hog-tied any women, whether in a month or a year or a lifetime.

"We're a sorry bunch of bachelors ourselves," someone finally declared.

Calvin swallowed the last of his dinner. "Well, misery loves company, I always say."

"Dell looks happier now," the younger man, the one whose idea it was to bet, observed. "At least, most of the time."

"You didn't see him this afternoon," Calvin replied. "A sadder sight never crossed the Lazy J."

"I thought you were gonna come up with a plan to make her leave."

"Yeah, well, I'm still thinkin' on it."

"You keep thinkin' any slower, and Dell will be

marching down the aisle and I'll be out fifty dollars," Cussy grumped.

Calvin got up and poured himself a cup of coffee. Cussy was right. He had to come up with a plan, and soon. Before his nephew—poor bastard—decided that married life was the answer to his prayers.

"ADVICE?" Mayme shrieked into the phone. "You want advice after you've been living on a stranger's ranch for eight days?"

"Well, I thought—"

"No," her friend interrupted. "You're not thinking at all. I can tell."

Allison almost laughed into the telephone. It was so good to hear a woman's voice after living with all these cowboys for more than a week. "My car is still broken. They have to rebuild the axle. Or something like that. I thought of a bus—"

"You can't take those tiny babies on a bus."

"That's what Dell said, too." She sighed, thinking of Dell's stunned expression when she told him she was leaving. And then he'd apologized, which made her feel worse. Especially since he really didn't have anything to be sorry for. She should have told him that during dinner. They should have talked about more than the weather.

"Well, he's right."

"He's asked me to decorate the ranch house. I'd already started helping him and now he wants to make it official."

"Make *what* official?"

"The job. But I'm not accepting his money, of course. If I stay."

"*If* you stay? Does that mean you want me to come get you?"

Allison hesitated. Of course that would be the sensible thing to do, but she didn't want to leave the ranch. She had come to think of this unexpected detour in Wyoming as a welcome vacation. She'd gone from having no one to help her with the babies to having two men willing to watch them and hold them and feed them once in a while. Just knowing there was someone else to help, if she needed help, eased the stress of being one hundred percent responsible for those little lives. The thought of leaving made her feel a little queasy. "I really don't want to leave. Not yet."

"Allison, is there something you're not telling me?"

She thought of Dell's kisses. "No. I don't mind staying here, that's all. I don't want to return to Kansas City. And I wanted to ask you what you thought."

Mayme was silent for several seconds. "Then stay there, I guess. It's better than being on the road alone with those babies, I suppose. You sound more rested, and if the men are helping with the babies—"

"They are," Allison assured her.

"And you're getting some sleep?"

"Every chance I get."

"Well," Mayme sighed. "I guess that's a good enough reason to remain on the ranch. You're not, um, romantically involved with your cowboy, are you?"

Allison pretended to find that funny. "Of course not," she said, and told her friend that the babies were fussing and she had to go. She said goodbye, replaced the telephone receiver, and returned the phone to its table in the hall. Romantically involved? She walked over to the set of windows on the other side of the dining room table. Dell was out there in one of the barns, but she had no idea what his chores entailed. He might have just made an excuse to leave the kitchen and leave her.

She'd assured him she would have no problems cleaning up the kitchen. She'd bathed, fed and readied the babies for bed as darkness fell and the lights came on in various outbuildings. She'd sat in the rocking chair and hummed "Home on the Range" until their eyes had closed and their breathing had grown even. The house was quiet, except for the occasional humming of the old refrigerator. Allison turned around and surveyed the large room. Tomorrow, she promised herself, she would find out what kinds of things Dell's father had stored in the shed. She would carefully paint a wall or two, polish the furniture and drape the log cabin quilt she'd found in the linen closet over the back of the couch. Painting last was doing the whole thing backward, but she was learning that here on the ranch, you did what you had to do with a minimum of fuss. Whatever it took to get the job done was done, without complaint and without talking it to death, either.

She'd piled newspapers, magazines and books on the front porch and didn't intend to tackle that part of the house until the main room was finished. She'd returned the unread serial killer mystery to the pile of hardcover books, too. There wasn't enough time to sleep, much less read.

And she'd rather spend that precious spare time helping Dell with the house or being outside. Maybe he'd ask her to ride with him again. Gertrude had been very polite and easy to sit on. She'd walked at just the right speed, as if she sensed that Allison wasn't ready to gallop all over Wyoming.

There were a lot of things she wasn't ready for, Allison decided, giving the back of the couch a pat to smooth the cushion into place. She wasn't ready to love again, so she shouldn't be thinking of kissing Wendell Jones. She should keep her mind on paint colors and furniture polish and washing diapers.

Mooning over a cowboy was strictly forbidden from now on. She went into the kitchen, found a pad of paper and a pen in one of the drawers, and sat down at the table to write a note for Dell.

"You have a deal," she wrote, and signed her name with a flourish.

"BLESS YOU," Dell said, after Allison's delicate sneeze. He carefully picked up a dust-coated chair and showed it to her. She stood closer than he would have liked, if he had his choice, but there wasn't much room in the crowded shed. And he held the only flashlight. He'd known, since he read her note last night, that she was going to stay awhile longer, and he'd slept well for the first time in many nights. "Is this the kind of thing you're looking for?"

She sniffed, sneezed again, and nodded. "That's one of the dining room chairs?"

"Yeah, I think so." He set it down and shone the beam of the flashlight across the pile of furniture to his right. "There are more of them here. How many do you want?"

"Six?" Her voice was hopeful, so he took a closer look.

"Looks like there are at least that many here." They were sturdy oak chairs that didn't look any the worse for wear, but he wondered if Allison realized just how much furniture polish it would take to make them look halfway decent.

"I think they'll be perfect. What's that over there, on your left?"

He swung light where she pointed and revealed some kind of cabinet. "I don't know what it is."

"Could it be a bookcase?"

"Maybe. Or a piece of junk. There's a lot of both stashed in here."

"Dell, you have no vision." She carefully climbed over a trunk to get closer to the piece of furniture.

He had a vision, all right, but it wasn't about arranging old pieces of oak in his living room. Allison's hair was piled on top of her head, revealing the back of her neck above the white T-shirt she'd borrowed from him. He wanted to touch his lips to that soft-looking strip of skin. He wondered if those wisps of golden hair would tickle his nose. She was so tiny that he could rest his chin on the top of her head while he pressed those womanly curves against his hard body. Dell watched her rub her fingers along the scrolled sides of the bookcase or whatever the hell it was, and longed for her to touch him. He would like to feel that touch once more.

But he'd given his word. And since she had stopped packing, he assumed she'd decided to stay. He would offer once again to pay her for her trouble.

"It looks like a Horta, I think. Or a good imitation of one."

"What's a Horta?"

"Victor Horta was a Belgian architect in the late eighteen hundreds. This is probably a very good copy of one of his trademark pieces, a buffet with cupboards at each end. See the scrolls on top? They'll be lovely once they're polished up a bit."

"It'll take four men to get it in the house," he commented. "Are you sure it will look good in the living room?"

She stood back and studied it. "I don't know why not. Those middle shelves give you a place for some books, and so do the glazed cupboards. You can hide your magazines in the cupboards underneath, see? It should hold a lot of your clutter, and be a real centerpiece for the room."

And must weigh hundreds of pounds. Why on earth had his father moved it out here in the first place? "Where?"

"Against the wall, to the left of the front door. We'll center it in the middle of that wall and it will be beautiful. The paint should be dry in another hour or two." She turned and smiled at him again, and Dell wondered if he would ever breathe again.

"How do you know all this?"

She grinned. "I took a class called European Furniture, 1860 to 1920."

"And got an A?"

"No, an A-plus." She shot him a quick grin and turned back to the piece of furniture.

"I should have known." He looked around the shop at the furniture piled to the ceiling. "Anything else you want out of here?"

"I could spend a week sorting through these things. Were they ever in your house?"

"They must have been. My grandmother was a wealthy widow from St. Louis when she met my grandfather. She must have brought this furniture with her, because she didn't want to leave her things behind. I think my mother had it all put away when she and Dad took over the ranch, after my grandparents died. She probably didn't want to have to worry about having anything fancy in the house. Calvin would know where it came from, if anyone would."

"It looks like it's in fine shape. I can't believe the glass isn't broken."

"Yet," Dell reminded her. "We've still got to get it back into the house."

"You won't let anything happen to it," she said. "You never do."

He pondered that statement while she investigated a worn footstool. "Has anyone in your family ever thrown anything away?"

"Not that I know of. Do you want the flashlight?"

"I'm trying to read the writing on this box." She blew at the dust but nothing happened, so she took the edge of her T-shirt and wiped the wood. Dell reached across an old table and handed her the flashlight.

"See if this helps," he said.

"'Marianna's Toys.'" She looked up at Dell. "Who is Marianna?"

"My grandmother." Dell tried to move closer, but didn't dare. His big feet would break something if he tried to climb over the furniture to see what Allison was looking at.

"Do you think we could open it?"

"Yeah," he said, curious himself as to what was inside the box. "I'll get it out with the rest of the things."

"Isn't this fun? Like a treasure hunt."

Or a challenge to his self-control, Dell thought, noting the way her jeans hugged her bottom when she bent to investigate something else. He was being tortured in the old storehouse and enjoying every painful minute of it. "Yeah," he muttered. "Fun."

The smile left her face. "I'm keeping you from your work, aren't I? I'm sorry, I should have—"

"No," he said quickly. "I have the time."

"Sure?"

"Yeah." He held out his hand. "Here. Let me help you get out of there. I'll come back with some of the men after lunch and we'll get this stuff out of here. If you're sure this is what you want."

"It'll look wonderful in that room, Dell. Really." She beamed at him as she took his hand and balanced on a low table, stepped over a couple of buggy wheels and landed against his chest when she tripped on a broken spoke.

He caught her with both hands and held her against him. He told himself it was just to stop her from pitching headfirst into a pile of old saddles, but he knew better. Her breasts were soft against his chest, the skin of her arms velvet under his hands. She smelled of lilacs and he could indeed touch his chin to the top of her head, but she looked up at him with those wide blue eyes.

"Sorry," he muttered, but he didn't release her. He was incapable of moving, as if his giant bulk had been frozen to the dirt-packed floor of the storehouse. If he lowered his head he could kiss her.

But he'd given his word.

"Dell?" she whispered, her voice sounding uncertain.

He didn't know if he should kiss her or toss her over his shoulder and take her to bed. Both actions would get him in trouble, but if she didn't move soon they were both going to be in a hell of a lot of hot water.

She didn't move. "I'm sorry about yesterday."

"Yesterday?" He blinked. What in hell had happened yesterday that she would be sorry for?

"Don't tease," she begged, looking up at him with that expression he never could figure out.

"Aw, hell," he muttered. He grasped her waist and lifted her up so that her lips were level with his. He kissed her for as many seconds as he dared, until the muscles in his arms started to burn with pain. Then he lowered her to the floor, but he kept his hands on her waist so she wouldn't run off before he said what he had to say.

"I broke my word, but dammit, sweetheart, you can't look at a man like that and not expect something to happen."

Allison looked a little dazed, but her arms crept around his waist and she lifted her face to his. "Stop talking and kiss me again."

He didn't need to be told twice. Her parted lips were sweet and inviting, and his tongue possessed her mouth with a longing and need that surprised even Dell. He kissed her thoroughly, until they both gasped for breath once he lifted his lips from hers, but he couldn't get enough. He held her tighter against him and took her mouth again while she held on to his belt as if to keep herself upright. The surrounding world, with its dusty furniture and rusted junk, faded away until Dell wondered how long it would take to swing her into his arms and carry her to the house. Doing that would mean having to stop kissing her for a fraction of time, and he wasn't prepared to do that yet.

A shadow crossed the open doorway. "What in the goldarn hell is going on in here?"

Dell broke off the kiss, but Allison's lithe body was still pressed against a part of him that enjoyed being pressed against. He held her waist and kept her there while he turned toward his uncle. "What is it, Cal?"

The old man looked disgusted, as if such goings-on in the storehouse were illegal or something. "I just came to tell you that the girlies are fussin' and prob'ly want their mama to come give 'em their lunch."

Allison pulled out of Dell's arms and didn't look at him. Instead she made her way through the clutter to the door, where Calvin stepped out of the way to let her pass. "Thanks for coming for me," she said.

"They're on the bunkhouse porch with Cussy," he said. "I haven't sniffed the house to see if that there paint smell has gone away."

"I'll take care of it," she assured him, and hurried off. Dell heard her footsteps in the dirt for a few seconds, then the only sound was Cal's huffing. Dell picked up one of the chairs and came toward the door.

"You gonna hit with me that cuz I spoiled your romantic morning?"

"I'd like to," Dell said, walking past his uncle and setting the chair outside. "But I've got five more of these to take to the house, plus some old cupboard and a box of toys. So I'm too busy to tell you to mind your own business, but if I had the time—" he shot Calvin a warning look "—I'd tell you to mind your own business."

"Humph." Calvin looked at the chair. "Haven't seen these in a long time."

Dell went into the shed and returned with another one, which he set in the dirt. "She likes them."

Dell gave Calvin a look that dared him to say anything before he went back into the shed. Calvin watched him silently, until six chairs and one old box sat outside of the shed.

"Now what?" his uncle asked, peering into the dark building.

Dell pointed to the cupboard. "See that? It's going into the living room."

Cal whistled. "Must weigh a ton. You'd better call some of the boys."

"Before we can get it out of there, I've got to clear a path first," he said, rolling up his sleeves. "And I might as well toss out some of the junk while I'm at it."

"You're not going to get rid of anything *good*, are you?"

Dell sighed. Calvin thought every bent nail and old plank ought to be saved, "just in case." "Tell you what, I'll just pile the stuff over on the side and you can go through it and see if there's anything you think is worth saving."

Cal looked relieved, and Dell smiled to himself. Sorting through junk would keep the old man busy and out of his way for the rest of the day.

"You're through kissin' that little gal for a while, then?"

Dell flushed and returned to the shed, but Cal followed him through the door. "You got no business with that little lady," he warned. "She'll be leavin' as soon as that car is fixed up and you'll be standing around with a broken heart for the rest of the summer and we all will have to look at your sad face."

"I've got some time."

"Meaning?"

"Meaning that car won't be fixed as soon as everyone thinks." He shot his uncle a warning look as he moved some tires from around the cupboard. "And don't you go blabbing that around, either."

Cal shrugged. "A man's gotta do what he's gotta do,

I suppose. And it's beatin' a dead horse to tell you to be careful, so I won't waste my breath." He peered into the gloom. "What the hell is that, your father's old anvil?"

"Yep."

"What's it doin' out here?"

"I don't know." He lifted it easily and moved it to another side of the shed. "There's enough stuff out here to outfit another house." He eyed the piece of furniture that Allison seemed so delighted with. It didn't look like much, but if it made her happy he'd haul it from here to California and back. Women were strange creatures, all right. Sometimes it didn't take much to make them happy; other times they needed the sun, moon and stars.

He turned to his uncle. "You gonna stand there gawking or are you gonna help?"

Calvin backed up. "You get hold of some of the younger boys, son. My days of bustin' a gut for a woman are over. And if I were you, I'd get on my horse and head to Texas while you still have a chance to escape."

"I don't want to escape." He wanted warm lips and a soft female body and he wanted the scent of lilacs to follow him around. She'd kissed him. She hadn't wanted him to keep his promise. She'd said she'd stay and fix up his living room. She'd had the room half-painted already, before he'd come inside at ten for that second pot of coffee.

He'd kissed her. She'd kissed him. They'd kissed each other. He didn't dare dream that there could be anything better than that.

PAINT FUMES. Dust. Lack of sleep. All of those things could cause her brain to clog so that she did something as foolish as kissing a cowboy in broad daylight, in an old shed, when she should have kept her mind on decorating. After all, that enormous Hortalike cupboard should have occupied her mind for at least ten or twelve hours. It wasn't often that a person entered a shed and came out with such an impressive piece of oak furniture.

Allison heated the bottles for the girls, who sat in their little car seats on the kitchen table and watched her with those now familiar expressions of curiosity and enjoyment. She would have sworn they knew exactly what she was doing and how long it should take before those bottles were in their mouths.

"Well, ladies," she said, putting her hands on her hips. "Your aunt Allison has gotten herself into another fix." The girls blinked, and Sylvie smiled. "Oh, go ahead and laugh," she told the baby, tickling her chin with one finger. "One of these days you're going to be all grown up and you'll think you know everything and then all of a sudden you'll be letting a cowboy pick you up and kiss you till you can't catch your breath and then things won't seem so hilarious."

Allison tickled Sophie, too, making the baby's lips turn upward. "You two better watch out for each other. That's what sisters do, you know."

"Is that what your sister did?" Dell asked, entering the room and taking off his hat.

"Well, she was five years older than me," Allison said, hurrying back to the sink to pull the bottles out of the hot water. She checked the temperature of the formula, glad to have something to do to keep from looking at Dell. "She was in college when I was in junior high. After our parents died, I moved to Kansas City to be with her." Allison didn't add that moving near Sandy was her idea, not her big sister's.

She took the bottles over to the babies.

"You need help?"

"No, thanks." She wished he'd leave. When Dell was around she was all too aware that she was attracted to him, which made life more confusing than she could handle. "I'm going to feed one at a time. Sometimes that works."

She lifted Sylvie from her chair and cradled her in her arms as she sat down at the kitchen table. Dell hesitated, then scooped up Sophie.

"No reason to make her wait," he said, taking the other bottle and putting it to the little girl's lips. He sniffed the air. "Paint smell is almost gone."

"I'll do the other half of the room this afternoon, while the girls are taking their nap. I'll keep the bedroom door shut so the smell doesn't bother them."

"It's a nice day." He walked over to the window and looked west. "You can open the windows."

*You can kiss me again.* Allison looked down at the baby in her arms and decided that she indeed had gone out of her mind. Round the bend and over the edge, definitely. She was now the mother of two. A month ago she had been engaged to marry someone else, and here she sat lusting over an oversize rancher who probably thought she was a candidate for Idiot of the Year. He walked into the living room and surveyed the east wall.

"Looks good," was all he said, but Allison was pleased with the compliment. She'd sketched out various arrangements for the furniture, and she liked the way the couch and chairs were arranged now. Of course, she'd pushed everything into the middle of the room so she could paint the walls.

"It will be finished in no time at all," she assured him. "And your life will be back to normal."

"I doubt it," he said, and she looked at him, but he turned his head away and said something to Sophie.

She doubted it, too. Allison turned back to the baby in her arms. After eight days on the Lazy J with Dell Jones, she didn't think any of them would ever be back to normal. She would miss him. They all would, of course.

Someday she'd tell them the story of how they moved to Seattle and ended up visiting a ranch in Wyoming, and how the cowboys took care of all three of them. She would send Christmas cards and pictures for a year or two. And someone would marry Dell, paint the walls a different color and get rid of the matching reclining chairs.

Allison sighed. It was too depressing to think about any longer.

THEY MANAGED TO AVOID each other. Of course, she didn't know if Dell was avoiding her, but it was a pretty good guess since he didn't come inside all afternoon. Allison played with the children, put them down for their naps, and picked up the paint roller. She was determined to finish painting the walls this afternoon, no matter how much the muscles in her arms would ache later on tonight.

Dell didn't come in for dinner either, though there was a pan of oven-fried chicken and foil-wrapped potatoes in the oven and a salad in the refrigerator. A loaf of Calvin's bread sat on a faded wooden board beside the sink, a serrated knife beside it. Allison served herself and ate alone. She glanced at the back door once in a while, but no one disturbed the quiet of the house.

Except the babies, who decided to be fussy and refused to go along with sitting in their seats and watching their aunt eat her dinner. They cried until tiny tears ran down their reddening cheeks, long after Allison gave up trying to eat with a baby on her lap, long after Allison gave up trying to eat dinner at all. She took turns walking each baby around the living room. She closed the windows against the night air, decided the paint fumes had dispersed, and sat down in the rocking chair with both babies in her arms.

They cried anyway. While Allison rocked the chair

in what she prayed would be a consoling motion, the little girls complained. She sang every song she knew, including a couple of campfire songs from her Girl Scout days. She told them stories about Cinderella and Snow White, making up the names of the dwarfs that she couldn't recall. She changed their diapers, looking for diaper rash, but there was nothing to see that could be causing either child to fuss with such gusto. She fed them, she burped them, she rocked them for hours, long after the sky darkened and sunset glowed from the west window. And long after Dell should have come inside for the night. Allison didn't want to admit that she missed him, missed their supper together, missed the hour when he would describe his day and tell about the calves and their mamas, or tell something funny one of the men had done. He would smell of the outdoors, of leather and hay; even after he showered Allison would swear she could still smell that wonderful leather scent.

The girls drifted off into sleep, but Allison was afraid to move and disturb them. Such peace was hard won, and therefore not to be tampered with. Allison, bracing her arms against the rocking chair's wooden armrests, managed to close her eyes and drift off to sleep, too.

DELL DIDN'T SEE her right away. Not until he'd switched on the light in the kitchen and noticed that the food was still sitting on the counter. It wasn't like Allison to leave a mess. He hung his jacket and hat on a peg by the door, then walked through the kitchen and peered down the dark hall. No light shone under the bedroom door. In fact, there were no lights shining anywhere.

Had she left? He felt his empty stomach drop to his

feet. Could Allison have been so upset with him that she took the children and left the ranch? She could have found the keys to any number of vehicles; they hung on a board over the washing machine. He turned right, into the living room, and heard the faint creak of the rocking chair on the wood floor. The furniture was bunched toward the center of the room, but off to one side was the rocker. Allison sat there in the darkness, her head resting on the back of the rocker, her arms full of babies. He didn't know how she slept without dropping the children, but as he came nearer he realized they were all asleep.

He wished they were his. He stood there for long moments and watched them. The little girls' faces were blotchy, as if they'd been crying. Allison's hair was loose and waved to her shoulders. She wore a pale yellow long-sleeve shirt and jeans, and her feet were bare. He wondered if she'd missed him at supper, or if she'd been happy to eat without him. Dell tiptoed backward out of the room, grabbed a piece of chicken from the pan, tossed the rest in the refrigerator, and went into his bedroom. He didn't want to wake up Allison and the babies, but on the other hand, Allison didn't look very comfortable and the girls should be in bed. He took a shower and was in the middle of putting on clean jeans when he heard the babies cry. He pulled a white T-shirt over his head and hurried out to the living room.

He would simply offer to help, he told himself, because any woman with an armload of crying babies certainly needed help of any kind, even from a clumsy cowboy who didn't know enough to quit while he was ahead.

"DELL?" Allison blinked and tried to remember where she was. Sophie and Sylvie were crying again, two off-key sopranos screaming for attention.

"Yeah," he said, his voice low. "Let me take one of them."

She felt Sylvie being lifted from her left arm and released her gratefully. She shifted Sophie against her shoulder and rubbed her back, but Sophie bobbed her head and screamed in her aunt's ear. "I don't know what's wrong with them."

"Hungry?"

"Maybe. What time is it?"

"After eleven."

"I'll fix the bottles. They were like this at suppertime, until they finally wore themselves out and went to sleep." Allison hid a yawn and stood, the screaming baby still against her shoulder. She took two bottles from the refrigerator, put them in a pan of hot water, then turned to Dell. "Could you carry Sylvie to the bedroom for me? I'll change them and see if that helps."

"Good Lord," Dell muttered, shifting the screaming twin from the crook of his arm to his shoulder. "She's real upset about something."

"I wish I knew what was the matter." She put the screaming Sophie on the bed and unsnapped the terry-cloth sleeper. Dell usually disappeared during diaper changing, but tonight he stayed in the room and laid Sylvie beside her sister. Allison changed each child quickly and handed one back to Dell. "Do you mind?" she asked.

"No. You think we should call a doctor?"

Allison went into the bathroom, washed her hands and splashed water on her face. From the sound of things it was going to be a long night. "I don't know what to do. I have a baby book. I can reread the chapter on crying."

Sylvie wailed an octave higher. "Good idea," Dell agreed, wincing.

She scooped up the sobbing Sophie from the middle of the bed, tucked her carefully in her arm and picked up *Child Care: The First Year* from the bedside table. "This is a pretty good book."

"It had better be," the rancher muttered, shifting Sylvie away from his ear. "She's gotta run out of air pretty soon, doesn't she?"

"I wouldn't bet on it," Allison said, hurrying toward the kitchen. "She and Sophie have more energy than I do sometimes, especially at night."

They tried giving the girls the bottles, which pleased them for only a few minutes. They cried around the plastic nipples and the milk dripped down the cheeks toward their ears and puddled in their necks. They burped and cried and carried on, waving little fists in the air and screwing up their faces to show their disapproval of everything around them.

"Good heavens," Dell sputtered, wiping his brow with a red bandanna. "It's midnight and they haven't given up yet."

Allison peered at the baby book. "The only thing I can figure out is that they're overstimulated, meaning their days have been so exciting that they can't get to sleep at night—"

"I can't picture that. Didn't they sleep on the porch with Cal this morning?"

"Yes. Wait a minute." She flipped ahead two pages. "Here it is. Evening colic? No, they're not acting like they have stomachaches."

"How do you tell?"

"They bring their knees to their chests. Let's see..." She ran down the list of things that could cause the babies to cry. "They're happier if they're being held, and they like to be rocked."

"I'll buy another rocking chair," Dell offered.

"Some babies like to be held, period. And then there's warmth." Allison tapped her finger on that column. "It says that some babies cry if they're not warm enough."

Dell eyed the blanket draped around the fussing child. "She looks warm enough to me."

Allison sighed. "They've been fed, burped, changed and snuggled. I guess all I can do is rock them and wait it out." She moved into the living room and sat down in the rocking chair. "Give me Sylvie and I'll do what worked before."

He waited for her to get settled in the rocking chair before handing her the second baby. She noticed he was careful not to touch her when he put Sylvie in her arms.

Dell straightened, taking a step backward. "I'll warm it up in here."

"Go to bed, Dell," she urged him. "I don't want to keep you awake, too." Besides, with Dell around it was only too easy to remember those kisses and the way those strong hands had lifted her up so he could kiss her. He'd made her feel delicate and fragile and desirable. Delicate and fragile she was used to, but desirable was rare enough to be tantalizing.

He left the room, and she heard the outside door shut. Within a few minutes he was back, his arms filled with firewood. The girls' tears had subsided, but they made tiny sobbing sounds every once in a while, as if to remind Allison that they still needed her to hold them. Allison watched as Dell arranged the wood, set a match to the kindling underneath, and the sticks burst into flame.

Dell looked over his shoulder at her. "It's worth a try," he said.

"Anything is," Allison agreed. She wished his shoulders weren't so broad, or his arms so strong. He was the kind of man a woman could lean on, the kind of man who'd driven wagon trains across the prairie and protected his family from harm. She longed to rest her head on that wide chest and sob her heart out, but knew if she did that she'd scare him into the next county. Dell avoided dirty diapers and weeping women, and heaven only knew what else. And she could hardly blame him.

She rocked the babies and enjoyed the fire, letting the warmth surround them. She felt herself relax, despite her careful grip on the children. Dell had bought a rocking chair large enough for triplets. Or one very large cowboy, she thought with a smile.

"Better?" he asked, clearing off a place on the couch to sit down.

"Much better," she assured him. She looked down at the babies, whose eyes had started to lose that miserable expression. "Right, girls?"

Sylvie sighed, a shaky little sound that tore at Allison's heart. "I wonder if they miss their mother. I wonder if they know that I'm not her."

Dell busied himself by pulling off his boots and tossing them aside. "What happened to your sister?"

"A car accident." It was still hard to believe, even when she said the words out loud. "She was driving to a doctor's appointment when a truck ran a stop sign and crashed into her. The babies were born a month early and Sandy didn't live to see them. And they never saw her."

"They're lucky to have you, Allison. That's real important to remember."

Allison held them a little tighter. "I'm the lucky one," she whispered, noting that Sophie's eyes had closed. "Even on nights when they don't want to go to sleep."

He leaned back against the back of the couch and stretched out his legs. The glow from the fire was the only light in the room, and it was enough for Allison to see Dell's profile, though she couldn't tell if his eyes were closed or open. She rocked gently for a long time, while the fire crackled and the man nearby kept her company. If he was asleep, she didn't care. She wasn't alone. She knew if she needed him she could call his name and he would help.

Dell Jones really was a special man. She shouldn't be so attracted to him. A woman with no home, no job and two babies had no business kissing anyone. Still, it was difficult to ignore the attraction she felt for the cowboy. He'd kissed her as if he'd desired her, but maybe cowboys who lived on remote ranches kissed women as if they were trying to turn them inside out. Maybe that was just part of living in the West.

He brought her a brandy without asking her if she wanted one. He set the glass on a table that he slid over beside her.

"Thank you," she said, knowing he didn't realize that she didn't have a free hand with which to pick up the glass. "I'll have to save it for later."

"I was going to offer to take one of the girls."

She shook her head. "I don't dare move them yet,

but thanks anyway." She looked around the living room and admired her painting job. "I'll fix the room tomorrow."

"The boys and I will bring in the cabinet, or whatever the hell it is, in the morning."

"I'll polish it," she promised. "You won't recognize it when I'm done. Do you want to arrange your own books on the shelves or should I do it for you?"

He sat down on the empty spot on the couch and took a sip of the brandy. "You can arrange anything you want."

"I want you to like it," she said, smiling a little. "That's the whole point, Dell." She didn't often say his name, and he looked at her with an unreadable expression on his big, familiar face. The flickering firelight threw shadows on his face. She was conscious of the quiet, of the fact that they were alone together after midnight, that there were only two babies between them. The knowledge brought a strange kind of tension and she wondered if Dell could feel it, too. Or if it was simply her imagination.

"They're quiet," he rumbled.

"They're asleep." She kept rocking, afraid to stop the motion and wake up the children. Their small bodies had gone totally limp, heavy with sleep. Their lips were parted in identical shapes, their breathing light and even. Allison knew they must be the most beautiful babies on earth. No matter what it had cost her to keep them, it had been worth it ten times over.

"I brought my grandmother's box to the front porch," Dell said.

"Were there toys inside?"

"I haven't opened it. I was, uh, waiting for you. We can open it in the morning, if you like."

"I'd like that. It must be wonderful to live in the same house all of your life, and to know your parents and your grandparents lived here, too. Not many people have that connection with their family's past."

"You didn't?"

"No. My father's job meant that we moved every year or two. There wasn't much time to put down roots anywhere."

"What kind of child were you?"

"A typical younger sister." She smiled, remembering how quiet the house had been after Sandy left. "A younger sister who was a little bit of a pest, but learned to mind her own business and tried to stay out of trouble. I grew up, went to college, got a job. After my parents died I decided to move to Kansas City to be with Sandy. There was no one left but the two of us and I wanted to be together."

"And your sister?"

"Had her own life. And her own ideas of how it should be lived. And that didn't always include a little sister."

"But you have her children."

"Yes." Her arms tightened around the sleeping babies. "I wouldn't let anything happen to them."

"Come on," he said, getting to his feet and crossing the room. He held out his arms. "Let me help you get them to bed."

"All right," she whispered. "Pick one."

Dell scooped Sylvie into his large hands with the experience of a father of ten, while Allison shifted Sophie with careful movements and followed Dell down the hall. They walked silently to the bedroom, the babies still sleeping in their arms.

"Here's the hard part," Allison whispered, facing

the girls' bed. "If we can get them down without waking them up, I'm going to deserve that glass of brandy."

Dell hesitated. "You go first."

She looked down at Sophie, who seemed to be almost unconscious with exhaustion. Allison could relate. She fiddled with the blanket, bent over and placed the baby carefully on the playpen mattress. The blanket went around her, too, and Sophie didn't open her eyes or complain in any way. "Your turn," Allison said, turning to the cowboy. "Or do you want me to do it?"

"Hell, yes." He handed Sylvie to her, and Allison managed to place the second child into the playpen without waking either her or her sister. They stood side by side and watched the babies for a long moment until, satisfied that the girls were going to remain asleep, Allison took Dell's hand and led him out of the room. She was halfway down the hall before she realized she held on to him so casually, as if holding his hand was the most natural thing in the world to do in the middle of a dark night. His skin was rough and calloused, his fingers gentle around hers.

This wasn't the first time she'd felt such a strong physical awareness of him, but it was the first time Allison found comfort in it. And something more. The firelight cast an intimate glow over the furniture pushed into the center of the room, and Dell picked up Allison's brandy glass and led her to the couch.

"You'll be warmer by the fire," he said.

She was altogether too warm already, but she sat beside him and kicked off her shoes, then tucked her feet underneath her on the couch. He handed her the glass and picked up his.

"To sleeping babies," he said, touching his glass to hers.

"And sleeping late," Allison added, and took a sip of the most expensive-tasting brandy she'd sampled. "If I'm very, very lucky they might sleep until seven."

He was still holding her hand. Dell lifted their joined hands and looked down at the joining. "This is all very strange," he muttered, then lifted his gaze to her face.

"Yes," Allison agreed, not pretending she didn't know what he was talking about. She tightened her fingers around his.

"Your coming here," he began, keeping his voice low while the fire crackled behind him. "Your *staying* here," he corrected, "was something unexpected. I never thought someone like you would come to the ranch."

"You brought me here," she teased. She wanted to throw her arms around him. She wanted him to kiss her again, the way he had kissed her in the shed. She wanted to run down the hall and lock her door before she made a complete fool out of herself. She kept her hand in his and took another swallow of her drink.

"Ah," he smiled. "That was one of my smarter decisions."

She finished her drink, letting the warmth seep into her bones and pool in her stomach, and set the empty glass on the floor. "Even with your living room in shambles and babies crying half the night?"

"Yes," he replied simply. "Even with babies and chaos. Because I've kissed you."

It was, Allison decided, the most romantic thing anyone had ever said to her. Mostly because Dell meant it, and because he didn't often say romantic things. He didn't often say anything at all. So when he tugged her closer to him, she went willingly. So willingly that it was a little embarrassing, but enfolded in those strong arms of his she felt safe, as she'd never felt so safe before. He smelled of soap and wood shavings. He was everything good and wonderful and solid. She put her arms around his neck and lifted her chin for his kiss.

She was growing accustomed to touching him, after all. His enormous size no longer frightened her. He held her as gently as he would a butterfly and he kissed her with the passion of a man who knew what he wanted was right in front of him. Allison found herself enfolded in an embrace that threatened to take her breath away. Not from the force of the man holding her, but from the intensity of feeling that took her by surprise. She'd expected comfort and instead there was that amazing longing to crawl inside Dell's skin.

He tasted of warmth and brandy. Somehow she was on her knees, to be closer to him. He released their clasped hands and wrapped his arms around her waist while he continued to kiss her.

Allison told herself later that it was inevitable. When Dell scooped her up into his arms and carried her to his bedroom, she was a happy woman. She was also a woman who was being kissed thoroughly the entire time it took to walk halfway down the hall to Dell's room. He nudged the door shut behind him, carried her to a wide bed and paused.

"Now would be a real good time to leave, if you're going to leave," he said. His eyes were dark as he looked down at her.

"No, thank you," Allison said, and kissed his chin. Which made him smile and drop her onto the bed.

"You can change your mind anytime."

"Do you *want* me to leave?"

"Hell, Allison, I'd be a fool to want you out of my sight," he muttered. He sat down on the bed and took her shoulders. "I'm not much of a ladies' man," he confessed.

"Good."

"I—mean," he stammered, "there've been a few women. But not here at the ranch. And not in a long time." His fingers swept across her cheek in the darkness, and he brushed the wisps of hair from her face. "And there's never been anyone like you."

"You don't usually talk this much," she murmured, placing little kisses alongside his mouth. "I thought you cowboys were men of action."

Even in the darkness she could see him smile. "Lady," he drawled, trailing one large hand gently across her breast, "you ain't seen nothing yet."

Allison inhaled sharply as his thumb caressed her nipple. She didn't know how her clothes came off, but together they managed to unbutton each other's buttons and unzip each other's jeans. It was crazy and right, and in the darkness of a Wyoming night all either of them wanted was to lie naked in a pile of sheets and make love for hours.

She climbed on top of him and buried her nose in the mass of dark hair that covered the largest chest she'd ever seen. She ran her hands along muscled arms, and those arms lifted her and then, with an agonizing slowness, lowered her on top of him. She was ready for him, even as big as he was.

He'd managed, sometime during the tangle of bodies and kisses and caressing hands, to put on a condom. He'd promised not to hurt her, worried that he would, and eased himself inside her with a control that made him grimace in pain and pleasure as he entered her sweet body. She was hot and wet and tight and he was afraid he would come inside of her at the very first thrust. But Dell knew that this miracle might never happen again, and he gathered every shred of self-control he possessed to prolong the lovemaking.

It was heaven and hell, all mixed up in a glorious tangle of silken hair and satin skin and the faintest trace of lilacs. He tumbled Allison onto her back, made love to her as if he would never make love to her again. Her climax caught him by surprise; he felt her tighten and contract around him, heard her sweet sigh of pleasure, and felt himself explode inside of her. He closed his eyes so she wouldn't see how deep the joy went. She didn't need to know that he loved her, though he longed to whisper the words into the soft skin of her neck while he made love to her again.

Dell was careful to rest his weight on his arms. He opened his eyes slowly, as the world settled back into place, to see Allison looking into his face. She touched his cheek, caressed the day's growth of whiskers, and smiled a tender little smile.

*I love you*, his heart pounded. *Love you, love you, love you.* The rhythm matched the thumping in his chest, but Dell was content to stay silent. He was either in love or having a heart attack from making love to an angel.

Either way, it didn't matter much.

When he thought he could move, he reluctantly withdrew from Allison's body and eased himself away from her. He grabbed a fistful of sheets and blankets, arranged them over their naked bodies, and gathered Allison into his arms. She snuggled against him, her head on his chest, until she drifted off into a sleep.

Dell listened to her even breathing while he counted his blessings.

ALLISON DIDN'T MEAN to kiss him in her sleep, but when she awoke a while later she was half on top of the naked rancher and shamelessly sprawled across his chest as if she were trying to crawl inside of him. She blushed when his eyes opened and he studied her with a curious expression.

"I'm sorry," she whispered. "I must have been dreaming. I didn't mean to bother—""

He took her face in his big hands and kissed her until they were both gasping for air and grasping for each other. She felt him hard against her thigh, leaving no doubt that there were some things she wasn't dreaming at all.

"Stay where you are," he ordered, his voice sleepy. "You're not bothering me." He chuckled as she blushed once again. "Well, not really," he added and reached for a condom.

She rolled to her side, and he rolled with her. He fit himself against her, entered her with a smooth stroke. His large hand splayed across her buttocks and held her tight against him while he moved inside her. Allison wrapped her arms around his neck, tossed her leg over his thigh and hung on. It was insanity to want him this much, but she did. And maybe she was just a little bit crazy.

He moved within her, again and again, creating sensations that made her gasp in pleasure. She kicked the sheet away; he tossed the blanket to the floor. He pulled her on top of him and rolled onto his back. Allison, perched above him, his body filling hers, felt as if she were making love to a giant.

It was a glorious feeling. She leaned forward and licked his neck.

10

"WHAT THE HELL is going on around here? The sun cleared the ridge an hour ago." Calvin's voice was an unwelcome intrusion on Dell's dream. "You sick or something?"

Dell kept his eyes closed and wished his uncle had stayed in the navy. Or better yet, had been stranded on a deserted island and forced to communicate by putting notes in bottles. He played dead and prayed Cal would lose interest and return to the kitchen.

"You ain't dead, are ya?" Calvin yelled.

Dell kept his eyes closed. "You'd be waking me up if I were."

"Coffee's on," his uncle said, "soon as you decide you can drag your sorry ass out of bed and do a day's work."

"You're gonna wake the babies," Dell cautioned. "They had a bad night, so quit yelling."

Cal lowered his voice, but kept talking. "Hell, the girlies have been up for an hour or more. Their mama fed 'em early. You're the only one around here still in bed with his eyes glued shut."

"All right. I'm getting up."

The bedroom door closed and Dell listened to the clunk of Calvin's boots heading toward the kitchen.

Dell rolled over, reached out and touched the empty space beside him. So it could have been a dream, he thought wearily, his eyes closed against the dim light of dawn. Except that his body was spent and if he wasn't tone deaf, he would surely break into song. He couldn't feel this damn good and have a dream be responsible.

Loving Allison had been real. He grew hard just thinking about the way his fingers had slid over that satiny skin, the way her legs had wrapped around his. She had been so delicate, and yet she had taken him inside her and turned his heart inside out.

He'd have to get out of this bed and find her. Or maybe not, he wondered, opening his eyes and surveying his empty room. She could have taken one look at him in the daylight and figured she'd made a big mistake. He scratched his whiskered chin and sat up. His room wouldn't win any prizes. A queen-size bed—the only new furniture he'd bought in twenty years—and a couple of old oak dressers were the extent of the decorations. He hadn't bothered with curtains for years and it was anyone's guess what the original color of the bedside rug had been.

Dell, naked and suddenly nervous, made his way to the bathroom. Hell, he'd shower and shave and get ready to bust his ass for the rest of the day, until he was too tired to think about Allison and her golden hair and soft skin and sweet-tasting lips, until he was too exhausted and bone-weary to wonder if Allison would come to his bed again tonight.

He wondered if he would be able to live without loving her again.

ALLISON DIDN'T KNOW if she was happy or disappointed that Dell wasn't in the kitchen when she fed the girls their early morning bottles. He was usually gone before the early feeding, then she put the girls back to bed and had some time to drink coffee, clean up the kitchen—if Calvin wasn't around to sputter—and shower.

This morning she'd managed to take a quick shower while the bottles heated up. The girls had been surprisingly patient and content to amuse themselves while waiting for breakfast and clean pants. Now they were fed and dry and still cheerful. Allison heard Calvin hollering at Dell to get up and quietly shut her bedroom door so the girls wouldn't cry for him. They seemed to like the old man; Allison swore they saved their best smiles for him. They seemed fine this morning, with nothing wrong at all. Allison sat on the edge of her bed and looked at them as they gurgled at each other in their playpen. If they would close their eyes, she could crawl—clothes and all—under the covers of her own bed and go to sleep.

Heaven knows she hadn't had much sleep last night. Allison smiled to herself and laid back on the bed. She had been made love to. Thoroughly, and with great passion.

She never would have suspected the big rancher would be such a lover. Of course, she hadn't had too much experience in that department. One brief fiasco in college had left her leery of young men with groping hands, and then much later there was Ryan. That had been a pleasant relief, but it didn't compare with what happened last night.

She didn't know how to explain last night. She couldn't blame it on the brandy, or the fire. She couldn't tell herself that she was lonely; who could be lonely taking care of twin infants? Allison closed her eyes and remembered Dell's large body filling hers.

She didn't know how to even describe what happened last night, even to herself. It must have been lust, because falling in love didn't happen in eight days. Except in books, or in romantic movies. This was no romantic movie. This was her life, and she had most likely screwed it up royally.

Allison drifted off to sleep, but not before wondering how on earth she would face Dell later on in the morning. She would hug him, she decided, because that would be a good way to show him that last night meant something special.

"ALLISON."

Allison opened her eyes to see Dell looking down at her, his beautiful mouth turned into a grim line. She tried to remember where she was as she struggled to sit up. "What time is—"

"Your fiancé's here." His voice was cold, the expression in his eyes wary. "I think his name is Ryan Conway?"

Allison blinked. "My fiancé?"

"You have one?"

"Ryan's *here*?"

He gave her a disgusted look. "Yeah, he's here, all right."

"In Wyoming?"

"In the living room."

"I can't believe this." She stared up at Dell and waited for him to tell her that this was a joke, but he turned away and headed for the door.

"You didn't answer my knock," he explained. "And I didn't want to wake the girls. Sorry for invading your privacy. Your *fiancé* said you were expecting him."

"He's not my fiancé, not anymore," Allison managed to say, but Dell had left and shut the door behind him with a quiet click. She looked over at the girls, whose cheeks were rosy with sleep, then glanced at herself in the mirror above the dresser. She smoothed her hair, tucked her shirt inside her jeans, and decided there wasn't time to find her shoes. Ryan Conway and Wendell Jones in the same room—in the same state, even—was something she had to see for herself.

Before Dell killed him.

Allison hurried down the hall and rounded the corner to see Ryan standing alone beside the rocking chair. The furniture was still pushed to the middle of the room, making the place look worse than it deserved to, although the dust-covered cabinet had been moved into place against the east wall. Dell had promised he'd have it moved in the morning, and there it was.

"Ryan?"

He turned around, his ivory windbreaker unzipped over a powder blue crew neck shirt. She'd bought him that shirt last Christmas, because it matched his eyes. He was tall and slender, with windblown light brown hair.

"Allison," he said, his handsome face breaking into a smile. "I was beginning to wonder if you were really here."

"What are you doing here?" She stopped four feet away from him and shoved her hands in her jeans' pockets. "How did you find me?"

"Mayme told me you were stranded on a ranch near Wells City. I stopped in town and asked directions."

She'd always thought he looked like Robert Redford's son, if Robert Redford had a son. She waited for the familiar thrill that seeing him brought, but nothing happened except strong feelings of annoyance and disbelief. "But why?"

"To see you, of course." Once again, that smile. He stepped forward and put his arm around her shoulders. "To ask you to come back."

"I've already moved away," she felt it necessary to declare, and stepped out of his embrace.

He chuckled. "You didn't get very far." He glanced around the room. "Redecorating, Allie?"

"Yes." Her chin lifted. "I've been hired to redo several of the rooms, plus a bunkhouse."

"A bunkhouse," he repeated, looking incredulous. "One of the most sought-after decorators in Kansas City is redesigning a bunkhouse?"

"I don't work in Kansas City any longer." Allison looked around for any sign of Dell or Calvin. Dell might stomp off and leave her with Ryan, but Calvin would have his hearing aid firmly in place and would take up a position in the kitchen so he could listen to every word being said.

"Could we talk about that? Maybe I was hasty."

"Hasty? You bought out my share of the business, Ryan. We signed the contracts Mayme drew up and you gave me a check." She stared up at him, trying to figure out why Ryan had come to Wyoming to find her.

"That can all be rectified."

"And the children?" She wondered how on earth he would have figured out how to deal with the babies. "What about them?"

"We'll hire a nanny. And we'll build a house. Didn't you always want to decorate your own house?"

"I always wanted a home of my own. That's different."

He looked around the room and frowned. "Could

we sit down somewhere and talk? I have a proposition for you."

"How about a cup of coffee? Come on."

She led him into the kitchen, where Calvin stood at the counter kneading bread dough. "Cal, I'd like you to meet Ryan Conway. Ryan, this is Cal Jones, the cook here on the Lazy J."

Calvin held out one flour-covered hand, and Ryan reluctantly shook it.

"Nice to meet you," the younger man said.

"Yep." The old man nodded, and Allison noticed his hearing aid was in place. "Who are you?"

"A friend of Allie's. From Kansas City."

Calvin turned back to his bread dough and pounded it against the wooden board. "What the hell are you doing in Wyoming?"

Ryan smiled, but Cal didn't see it. "Trying to talk Allie into coming home with me. It was good of you to give her a place to stay on your ranch."

"Ain't my ranch." It was said with great belligerence.

Allison decided against the coffee and steered Ryan back toward the living room.

"Whose ranch is it?"

"Mine," Dell said, standing in the doorway. He held both babies in his arms and his expression was deliberately bland. "I'm Dell Jones, owner of the Lazy J." He turned to Allison. "They were crying."

Ryan looked surprised, then chuckled. "*You*'re Dell Jones?" He turned to Allison. "You wouldn't believe what a waitress in the café told me."

"And what was that?" Dell planted his feet on the floor and held the silent babies with steady arms.

Ryan shook his head, obviously rethinking what he

was going to say. Allison could guess. Lucille must have been flapping those red lips of hers. "Never mind." He turned to Allison. "Is there someplace where we can talk privately?"

Allison wished Dell would look at her. She wished he'd smile or wink or something, just to show he didn't believe that she would make love to him while she was engaged to marry someone else. She ignored Ryan's question. He hadn't acknowledged the children or asked how they were doing. All he could think of was hiring a nanny and resuming life as usual. "I'll take the girls," she said, stepping closer. "They must need to be changed."

"Yeah," Dell said. "I'll take them back to the bedroom for you."

She turned back to Ryan. "Have a seat. I'll be back in a few minutes."

He grimaced, barely glancing at the babies. "Guess some things don't change."

Allison ignored him and followed Dell down the hall and shut the bedroom door behind her. "He's not my fiancé," she said to Dell's broad back. He set one girl, then the other, on the bed.

"Then why does he think he is?"

"He *was*. Once. Before the babies came."

Silence. He moved aside so she could unfasten the girls' sleepers. Neither Cal nor Dell had ever stayed in a room where there was diaper-changing going on, so Allison figured the silent rancher was willing to listen to her. "We were partners in a decorating business. He specialized in business environments and I did houses. We were engaged for two years, living together for six months, and then the babies came. And Ryan left."

Which, she wanted to add, was exactly what the girls' father had done, too.

Dell cleared his throat. "Why?"

"Why did he leave?" Dell nodded, a grim expression clouding his face. "He didn't want children. At least, he didn't want someone else's children. He didn't like the noise or the mess or the fact that I wanted to stay home and take care of them and not display carpet samples anymore." Allison swallowed hard, hoping to dislodge some of the bitterness she heard in her own voice.

"You loved him."

"Yes. At least, I thought I did." Looking back now, she wondered if the marriage would have worked. They most likely would have done fine, unless she decided that what she wanted was different from what Ryan wanted.

Ryan usually got what he wanted.

Allison changed the diapers slowly, giving Dell as much time as she could to say something. Anything. She would have settled for a smile or a pat on the back. A brief kiss would be nice, too. But the stubborn rancher simply leaned against the wall, his arms folded across his chest, his gaze on a spot above the headboard.

"Would you watch them while I wash my hands?"

He nodded, so Allison gathered up the dirty diapers and went into the bathroom. When she returned, Dell was sitting on the bed tickling Sylvie's chin. He stopped when she stepped into the room.

"What does the son of a bitch want now?"

"To take me back to Kansas with him."

"And the girls?"

"I don't intend to go anywhere without the babies."

Dell nodded. "Yeah, I can see that. You think *he* will?"

She wanted to touch him. She wanted to stand in front of him and put her hands on either side of his face and kiss those frowning lips of his. She wanted to kick him in the shins and make him beg for mercy. "Move over," she said, her voice brusque. "I can't stall in here much longer."

He moved, and she sat down beside him on the bed. Their thighs touched, but neither moved to break the contact. "I'm not going back with him."

"I wouldn't blame you if you did."

Allison turned sideways to face him. He looked as if he'd blame her for the rest of her days if she walked out that door this morning. She touched the back of his hand. "You must have chores to do."

"Are you trying to get rid of me?"

"I'm trying to tell you that I have to talk to Ryan. He came all this way. It's the least I can do."

"Yeah, well." He shrugged and moved off the bed. "He doesn't want the girls?"

"No." And he never would, no matter how hard she tried, Ryan was not ready, willing or able to be a father. When it came right down to it, no one was.

Dell picked up Sophie, who started to cry. "He can stay for lunch."

"Thank you." She gathered up Sylvie, who was about to burst into tears, too. "I guess everyone's hungry."

"We'll feed 'em," Dell said. "All of 'em, and then maybe we'll have some peace around here."

"And I've got some furniture to move," Allison said, suddenly feeling more cheerful. "I can't keep you in a mess." She opened the door and headed down the hall.

Ryan could talk until he was blue in the face, but that wouldn't change anything. She wasn't going back to business as usual.

"I NEED YOU, Allie. I've fired three assistants in three weeks." Ryan put his hands on his hips and surveyed the living room furniture. "Tell me you're not going to keep that sofa."

"I'm putting a quilt on it."

"A *large* quilt, I hope." He helped her push the green recliners into place by the east wall. "These hideous things should have been banned years ago."

"They're comfortable, and the men like watching football."

Dell almost said something, like *get the hell off my property*, but Allison didn't seem to be bothered by her ex-fiancé's comments, so he leaned against the doorway of the kitchen and watched the two of them move the furniture into place.

"Where on earth did you find that cabinet?"

"The Horta? Out in the shed."

The clown from Kansas shook his head. "It's not a Horta. Not enough detail on the scrolls. And the wood is all wrong."

"You sure?"

"Positive. But it's a nice piece all the same. Made in New York, not Belgium." He turned away from the cabinet and surveyed the rest of the room. Dell watched to make sure he didn't lay a finger on Allison. He expected the man to keep his distance or pay the consequences.

"Don't you have somethin' better to do?" Calvin asked, coming up behind him.

"Nope."

"You've been standin' here for an hour. You think she's gonna fall into his arms if you're not standin' here to make sure she doesn't?"

"I'm making sure he doesn't try anything."

Cal shook his head. "You've been acting pretty strange, son. Sleepin' late don't agree with you."

Dell thought about what had happened last night and wondered if his uncle was right. Making love to Allison had agreed with him, all right. It was just the morning that had been tough to take. "That slick bastard isn't going to take Allison away with him."

"You don't have a choice, Dell. That ain't up to you."

"It should be," he growled. He had tasted heaven last night and this morning he was chewing dust. His fists were clenched tight and he wanted to pound something, but Allison wouldn't like it if he messed up her guest. Hell, he'd been the idiot who had invited him to stay for lunch. The man had been personable and charming, grateful for the invitation and curious about the ranch. He'd eaten Dell's beef and thanked Calvin politely for the meal.

And Dell, sick with visions of that man making love to Allison, wanted to stomp him into the shape of a cow pie.

"But it ain't up to you." Cal patted him on the shoulder. They watched Allison and her friend argue over the placement of the couch as if they'd argued over furniture a thousand times before. "She's not yours, Dell. She's a woman with a broken car and two babies and she's not gonna stay here on this old ranch takin' care of a bunch of sorry cowboys."

"Shut up," Dell said, his voice deadly quiet. He watched Allison stand beside the handsome blond man. They made a good-looking couple, like a magazine advertisement for toothpaste or vitamins or yuppie running shoes. Yellow hair and blue eyes, perfect in every way.

Except, Dell thought in grim satisfaction, Conway didn't want the babies. And Wendell Jones, big ugly cowhand that he was, did. He wanted Allison, too. And she was here, her car being repaired slowly and painstakingly by a guy whose freezer was going to be full of beef come fall. He'd had ten days to show her what her life would be like if she stayed. He'd thought he'd had a chance, until Conway showed up with his offers of business deals and nannies and a new house.

Dell turned his back and walked through the kitchen, picked up his hat and left the house. Maybe it was time to give up. A smart man knew when he'd been beaten.

"LAST CHANCE," Ryan said, smiling that charming smile of his. The blue eyes looked a little sad, though. He waved his arm toward the ranch buildings. "I could still take you away from all of this."

Allison kissed his cheek and took a step away from the car. "Thanks, but I'm going to stick with my original plan."

"Looks like you've gotten sidetracked."

"Temporarily," she insisted, knowing sooner or later she'd have to leave the safety of the ranch.

He hesitated before getting into his car. "We could have made it work, I think. I do love you."

She shook her head. "You don't want the babies, Ryan. You never did, and our staying together and raising them isn't fair to them or to you. Sooner or later it would have fallen apart."

"Well, I'm sorry about that." He grimaced. "Babies

and diapers and bottles are a bit much. And if I ever decide to have a child, I want him to be my own."

"I know," Allison said, wishing he would just get in his car and leave. She felt as if the children had been rejected once again, but at least she knew now, without the smallest doubt, that she had done the right thing by starting over. The girls would never have to find out that "Uncle Ryan" would prefer they talk to the nanny, that their father didn't want them, that their half-brother and half-sisters lived in the most expensive section of town and didn't know the twins existed.

He got in the car, started up the engine and within a few minutes was just a cloud of dust on the long drive to the main road. *If I ever decide to have a child, I'd want him to be my own.* The words echoed in Allison's head as she walked up the steps to the front porch. She tiptoed down the hall and checked on the sleeping girls. She'd done the right thing by leaving, but now what? She was in danger of falling in love with the big rancher, and there was no reason to believe that Wendell Jones was interested in anything more than a brief affair. He was the kind of man she could love with her whole being, depend on till her dying day, trust with her heart.

She didn't know whether to run into his arms or hitchhike to town to buy a station wagon.

THE IDIOT COWBOY didn't come inside for supper. Allison picked at her food, oven-fried chicken and baked potatoes, until she pushed the plate aside. She couldn't leave the babies alone while she searched the ranch for one Wendell Jones and the man knew that.

Allison waited for Dell, knowing he'd have to come inside eventually. The girls were tired tonight and easily went to bed after baths and bottles. She cleaned up the kitchen and watched out the window as lights glowed in the outbuildings. The men would be gathering around the scarred oak table for their nightly games of cards and Scrabble. Cal told her he was the ranch champion. She didn't know whether to believe him or not.

It was after ten when Dell entered the kitchen. He looked tired, which was no surprise. Neither of them had gotten much sleep last night.

He glanced in her direction, took a glass from the cupboard and poured himself a drink of water.

"Long day?" Allison asked.

"Yeah." He drained the glass in one long motion, then refilled it and leaned against the counter. "Real long."

He was jealous, Allison realized. He actually thought that Ryan could snap his fingers and she'd grab the girls and the diaper bag and go running back to Kansas. She didn't stop to wonder why she was pleased that Dell was acting this way. She waited for him to ask where their visitor had gone. "More calves today?"

"Just a few. Nothing to speak of. The season's over, 'cept for the surprises." He took another drink of water and gave her a level look. "Speaking of surprises, where's Conway?"

"In Cheyenne, I guess."

"Heading east?"

"Yes."

"Without you?"

"Yep." She waited for a reaction, but didn't get one. Dell stood quiet and calm, drinking his water. They may as well have been talking about the weather. Had she imagined the flicker of jealousy?

"You were together a long time."

"Yes."

"Shouldn't you be crying or something?"

"Not if I'm not sad." She stood. "I called the garage today and checked about the car. He said to give him another week."

"A week," he muttered, setting the empty glass in the sink as she crossed the kitchen to stand in front of him. Allison put her arms around his waist and looked up into his face.

"Seven days. Do you mind?"

"No."

His arms started around her, then stopped. "I'm dirty and covered with—"

"That doesn't matter," she said, laying her head on his chest. "I just need you to hold me." She needed him for a lot of things, but she wouldn't tell him so. She would stay for seven more days. She would wrap her arms around him and show him that he shouldn't stay up here alone on the ranch for the rest of his life. She would teach him to dance and show him that he was attractive and help him get out of his isolated rut.

"You smell like furniture polish," he said, wrapping her into his embrace.

And she would love him, Allison added to her mental list. Heaven knows, he was a man who deserved it.

11

MIDNIGHT FOUND HIM lying naked, Allison tucked against his chest. Her hair was spread across Dell's shoulder, the curls tickling his neck. He thought he might have dreamt the past hour, except she was soft and warm against him. She'd taken his hand and led him into the bedroom. They'd showered together and she'd scrubbed his back. He took her to bed and kissed that lovely body in places that drove them both crazy with desire. When she'd taken him inside her body, the pain of the day had receded and Dell had realized that he'd been given the gift of another night.

Allison lifted her head and kissed his mouth.

"Smile," she commanded, looking down at him. "You haven't smiled at me all day."

He hadn't felt like smiling. He'd felt like drowning himself in the old horse trough behind the barn when he'd seen that handsome son of a bitch grinning down at Allison. Dell knew damn well that the Conway character wasn't worthy of Allison and she was better off without him, but he was sure surprised that Allison knew it, too.

She continued to look at him. "You're still not smiling."

"Sorry." He forced his face into what he hoped was a pleasant expression. "That better?"

"Mmm." Allison tilted her head and didn't look impressed. "I'm sorry about today."

"There's nothing to be sorry for." It wasn't her fault that Conway found his way to the ranch.

"You didn't get a chance to look at the living room, did you?"

"No."

She nodded. "That's what I thought. Tomorrow you can tell me if you like it or not."

"It'll be fine." He closed his eyes so she wouldn't see the love he felt. There was no sense in acting like a lovesick fool.

"Do you want me to leave?"

"Leave?" He opened his eyes and studied her face. He thought they'd settled that. She would stay for another week and he would try like hell not to make a fool of himself.

"Calvin came to your room this morning. I don't want him to find me here tomorrow."

"That was because I didn't get up. Stay," he said, tightening his arms around her. "I'll set the alarm clock."

"I have to open the door so I can hear the babies. They'll never sleep through the night since they went to bed so early."

"We can sleep in there," he offered.

She shook her head and his heart sank until she added, "Not if we're not going to sleep." She smoothed the palm of her hand along his chest, then lower. Her small fingers found him, then hesitated. "And I don't think we're going to sleep right away."

He shook his head and felt himself grow larger against her fingers. "No."

Allison caressed him with her hand until he thought

he would disgrace himself by passing out from the pleasure. She'd never touched him so deliberately before. After several of the most enjoyable minutes he'd experienced in his life, Dell rolled Allison onto her back. She wound her arms around his neck.

"You're smiling now," she told him.

"Am I?"

She nodded and kissed his chin. "Now I know the secret."

"I am making love to a very smart lady."

"And a very happy one," she added.

Dell paused. "Are you, Allison? Happy, I mean?"

"Yes." Her hand caressed his face. "And happiness is a welcome change from the past months, believe me. I'm glad it was you who rescued me."

He entered her with a single stroke, feeling that sweet, tight warmth encompass him. Her arms tightened around his neck and he heard her gasp as he moved within her. He moved slowly, prolonging the sensations, until neither one could delay the inevitable climax that swept them both.

When Wyoming settled back to earth and Dell remembered his name and other details of their conversation, he gathered Allison into his arms. "I'm glad I rescued you, too," he lied, though a sinking feeling accompanied the words. Calvin was right. Allison was going to break his heart. He was a goner, all right. He'd fallen for the first pretty woman to enter the Lazy J and now she was in his bed and her babies were down the hall.

She would move on to Seattle and marry a guy who looked like that Conway character. They would have beautiful babies who would wear booties, not boots.

He would never see the girlies again, or feel Allison's skin against his.

He'd learned a lesson today, Dell decided, and it had nothing to do with making love or figuring out where the couch should sit.

"HOW ARE THINGS in the big house?" Cussy called as Cal made his way across the yard. Cussy was saddling up his horse and preparing to check fences in the western hills. "Who's gonna win the bet?"

Cal lifted his hat, scratched his head, and replaced his hat low on his forehead. "Don't rightly know. Things are sure heatin' up." He hadn't liked what he'd seen this morning. Dell had that tired look again, yet he didn't seem sick. Allison had blushed her morning greetings while she fed the girlies.

"You got the inside track, Cal. We heard her old boyfriend came to visit."

"Yep. He wanted her back but she sent him packin'."

"Yeah?"

"Yep. She made him help her move all the furniture first, though. Smart gal, that one."

"Smart enough to know a good man when she's found one? The boss could use a wife."

Calvin shrugged. "She ain't ranch material. Hell, she's painted the walls and moved my chair."

"You'll get over it," the cowboy said. "And you like them babies."

Cal couldn't deny that. Them girlies were a lot of fun, and as long as no one expected him to change diapers he was happy to sit with them and read his magazines. He'd collected quite a piece of change, too, with all the baby-holdin' goin' on, too. "Don't know what they'd do without me," he boasted.

Cussy gave him a solemn nod. "Damn right. You'd make one hell of a grandpa, that's for damn sure."

"Grandpa?" He stared at the other man, who had swung himself onto his horse and gathered the reins. "*Grandpa?*"

"Well, isn't that what you'd be if Miz Allison stuck around?"

Calvin scratched his head as Cussy trotted toward the fence line. A grandfather. He hadn't thought of that. 'Course, Dell had been like a son to him. Always had. He'd never figured Dell for a family man, so he'd expected the two of them would go on as they always had. He turned and gazed toward the house. So little Allison was blushing and Dell had circles under his eyes. That could only mean one thing.

There was more goin' on in the ranch house at night than midnight bottles.

Which meant the girlies might leave or the girlies might stay. Could be trouble either way, Cal figured.

Hell, now he had to do some more thinkin'.

"WHAT DO YOU THINK?" Allison waved toward the living room and waited for Dell's reaction. He surveyed the cabinet that she'd turned into a bookcase, the antique quilt that covered the back of the couch, the dining room chairs that surrounded a gleaming table.

"Real nice." He took a step backward, into the kitchen, and poured himself a cup of coffee. Cal looked up from kneading dough and gave Allison a wink.

"Real nice," he said, echoing his nephew's words. "I can still see the TV from my chair."

"I'm glad." She turned toward Dell, who didn't look at her. She told herself she shouldn't be disappointed. She knew he was a man of few words, but she'd expected a little more than "real nice." "You don't like it," she said, following him to the kitchen table. The girls gurgled and kicked from their car seats, but Dell didn't seem to notice.

"I like it just fine."

Maybe he was disappointed that she hadn't hung the gold mirror in the living room. She'd debated about returning it, but put it in the bathroom instead where it brightened up the small area. "I saved the little pink dresser for the front porch," she said, trying to get his attention. "I might paint it forest green and do the porch in green and white."

Dell nodded. "All right."

Allison wiped a dribble from Sylvie's chin and watched as Dell moved to the sink. He poured his coffee down the drain and set the mug on the counter. She wouldn't have thought this was the same man who made love to her two nights. Twice. He'd withdrawn since then, as if he were trying to distance himself from her and the children. Yesterday she'd been too busy with the babies and the decorating to take it personally. She'd slept in her own bed because he was late at the barn, but this morning he was avoiding her. And that hurt.

She tried one more thing because before he escaped outside into the bright spring sunshine, she wanted to finish the living room. "Would you mind if we opened the box?"

He frowned. "The box?"

"One of the men brought it in with the cupboard and the chairs. It's the box of your grandmother's toys."

"Go ahead."

"You don't want to see?"

He hesitated. "No. Go ahead. Surprise me."

"Okay."

"Nice day," Cal declared, looking out the window at the cloudless sky. "S'posed to be a good weekend, too."

"Thanks for the update," Dell muttered, heading for the door.

"Kelly Beatrice called. She wanted to know if you could donate a hundred dollars toward the raffle. I told her, hell yes. Don't you always?"

"Fine." He grabbed his hat.

"She wanted to know if you and Allison here would be going to the May shindig on Saturday, and if you wanted to sit with her and Jack for supper. I told her yeah, that was fine. You're to meet them there at six o'clock."

Allison turned to Dell. "What's going on?"

His gaze flickered over to her. "May Days. Used to be a party after calving season. Got out of hand."

"Raises a nice chunk of money, too," Calvin added. "Just about everyone in the county shows up." He turned to Allison. "I'll take care of the girlies, of course. I'll get Cussy to help."

"I haven't been invited," she pointed out.

"Aw, hell, you're going with that grouchy nephew of mine. And it's potluck. You're s'posed to bring a dish. And then there's the dancin'." He winked at her. "Figures that now that Dell can dance, he oughta take you to town and show off a little bit."

Dell glared at him, but Cal didn't seem to notice. He turned back to his work and kept kneading that dough until it was silky and smooth. "I'm not making a fool of myself in front of the whole town," he declared.

Allison smiled at him. "It would be fun to go," she mused. "We wouldn't have to dance."

"Hell."

"Unless you already have another date?" In which case, she'd have to do something drastic, like tie him up in the barn so he couldn't go to town and dance with anyone else but her.

He shot her a disgusted look, jammed his hat on his head and left the room. She heard the back door bang shut, then watched out the window as Dell crossed the yard and headed toward the barn. She didn't envy the men who had to talk to him today.

She left the window and turned to Calvin. "What kind of dish?"

The old man shrugged. "I usually bake up a few pans of rolls, but since this is your first time you oughta bring something yourself. You have any favorite recipes?"

"Not exactly."

Calvin, a pained expression on his face, sighed. "Guess I'll have to teach you something then."

HELL AND DAMNATION. He'd been roped into going to a goddam dance. Here he thought he was doing such a good job at staying away from her, and now he was taking her to town. Dell glared at himself in the bathroom mirror and parted his damp hair with the comb. He'd been trying to act civilized by not making love to her every night. And he'd managed to avoid his bed for two long nights, but there'd be no helping him now. After an evening of looking at Allison and breathing in her perfume and dancing with her, he'd have a hard time walking to the truck without embarrassing himself.

Dell sighed and adjusted his string tie. He wanted her all the time. He wanted her beside him when he rode out to check the cattle or talk to the men. He wanted her across the supper table. He wanted to drink his morning coffee and watch her feed the girls. He liked the way she teased him and he liked his new living room.

He was a sorry lovesick mess of a man. Anyone in town tonight would see that right off. They would point and say, "There goes old lovesick Jones, dancing over there with the beautiful blonde."

And someone else would say, "Wonder what the hell she sees in him." And no one would have an answer. Not even the guy they were talking about.

"You ready yet?" Cal hollered.

"Almost." Dell stuck his head out of the bathroom as his uncle approached.

"The little gal is out in the kitchen with the girlies." Cal surveyed his polished boots, pressed slacks and white shirt. "You look right nice. Better 'n usual."

He winced. "Thanks."

"I see you've got your dancin' shoes on."

"Yeah, for what it's worth. I'm gonna look like a fool."

"You're gonna look like the luckiest man in the county," Cal assured him. "The little gal looks real pretty, and she's made your favorite food."

"Apple pie?"

"Nope." Cal looked disgusted. "Enchiladas. I gave her the recipe and taught her how."

Dell's mouth dropped open. "You gave her a recipe? You let her cook in your kitchen?"

His uncle shrugged. "Yep. So what?"

He brushed by him and took a sport coat from the closet. "Just wondering if you were feeling all right, that's all. Guess you're getting soft in your old age."

"She's a nice little gal. Mebbee I was wrong about her. About women. Mebbee you should sweet-talk her into stayin' around here, be on your best behavior tonight, dance real nice."

Dell shook his head. "I feel like I'm going to my own funeral."

"What the hell are you talkin' about? You're goin' to the supper dance with the prettiest gal in Wyoming. You'd better perk up, son."

"People are going to wonder what she sees in me."

"You always were sensitive about your looks." Cal shook his head. "You've grown into that nose, and all that weight on you is pretty much muscle. It ain't as bad as you think. And the little gal seems to like you."

Dell closed his eyes against the vision of a naked Allison sliding on top of him. Yes, she seemed to like him, but there was a world of men out there. He opened his eyes and forced himself to face reality. "She could have her pick of any man in Wyoming, and you and I both know it."

Calvin winked at him. "But it looks like she's picked you, son. If I were you I'd quit bellyachin' and start enjoyin' life. You ain't the prettiest cowhand around, but you're a decent man, with a good head on your shoulders and not a mean bone in your body. That little gal should thank her lucky stars you came along when you did."

"You're not kidding me, are you?"

"Not about this," Calvin said, his voice solemn. He fiddled with his hearing aid. "Sure glad I got to wearin' this contraption. I kinda like this baby-sittin' job."

"They're a handful. Is Cussy coming over to help?"

"Yeah. We're gonna watch the fights and I'm gonna stick him with changin' diapers."

Dell shoved his wallet into his back pocket and took a deep breath. "I guess we're ready then."

"Yep." Cal gave him a pat on the back that threatened to shove him out into the hall. "You go on now, and show that little gal a good time."

"DANCE?" Dell asked, standing and taking her hand in his.

Allison smiled. She'd been hoping he'd quit looking nervous every time the band played a slow song. "Sure."

He led her from their table and onto the dance floor, the center of the community center where a large crowd of people of all ages were dancing. He took her into his arms and managed a respectable two-step around the dance floor.

"Anyone looking?" he asked.

"Just Lucille. She's green with envy because I'm dancing with you and she's not." She smiled up at him. "I'm glad you're dancing."

"Yeah, until I step on your foot and cripple you for life."

"I'll take my chances."

He held her closer, and Allison pretended that she belonged here, in Wells City, Wyoming, population 8,243. She wondered what it would be like to shop for groceries and run into friends. She would like to know some other mothers and take the girls to preschool in a few years. She'd like to drive carpools and learn to bake and ride a horse as calm as Gertrude.

Everyone had been so kind tonight. The enchilada pan had been scraped clean by seven o'clock. Dell, unaware that she had made the casserole herself, had two helpings. Kelly's husband, a lean rancher with an easy smile, also went back for seconds, so Allison was pleased that she hadn't hurt Cal's reputation as a cook. She'd brought a couple of plastic bags filled with homemade rolls and delivered them to one of the ladies working behind the serving tables.

"I still can't believe how you know everyone. I've never lived in a small town like this. No wonder you don't want to leave."

"Most everyone has asked me if you're the same gal who's living with me."

"Uh-oh."

He looked down at her and chuckled as the music stopped. "You brought it on yourself, you know, by teasing Lucille the way you did."

"She deserved it." She waited for him to release her, but he only tightened his hold as the band started to play a waltz.

"I can waltz," he informed her. "It might be my one and only accomplishment."

She gave him a wicked smile. "I think you have a few others." When he winked at her, she blushed. The couple beside them laughed.

"Lady, are you flirting with me?"

"I'm allowed. After all, I'm your date, aren't I?"

"Yes," he murmured, holding her tighter. "You sure as hell are."

Allison liked his reaction. They danced in silence, and every once in a while Allison could hear Dell counting under his breath. When the music ended, he released her, touching her back to guide her back to the table.

"Speak of the devil," he said.

"Who?" She couldn't see through the crowd.

"Your favorite waitress. Be nice."

"I'll be nice as long as she's nice to you."

He gave her a warning look, but his dark eyes twinkled. "Don't start trying to kiss me. I'm not going to fall for that one again."

His hand tightened around hers and Allison chuckled as they neared the table. Lucille, in a bright green Western shirt, looked up from her conversation with Kelly's husband and smiled.

"Hey, there," the redhead drawled. "You through dancin', Dell? I didn't know you had it in you."

"Allison's been giving me lessons." Dell pulled out a chair and Allison sat down on the other side of Jack Beatrice. She planned to stay as far away from Lucille as possible. If Dell wanted to dance with her, he was welcome to and she wouldn't do anything to embarrass him. After all, now that he was becoming more social, he might meet someone he'd like to date. Allison decided she wouldn't think about that. The big rancher sat down and Jack handed him an unopened bottle of beer and Allison retrieved her plastic cup half-filled with white wine, from the center of the table.

"Where's Kelly?"

"Calling home to check on the kids," her husband said, stifling a yawn. "We've become old fogies now."

Dell turned to Lucille. "You want a drink, Lucille?"

"Pete's bringing me one, thanks." She turned to Allison. "He has some good news for you."

"About my car?"

Dell nodded at the group of people still dancing. "Good turnout this year. How much money do you think it made?"

"Plenty," Jack said. "More than last year, I'll bet. How'd you make out this spring? Never saw such weather."

Allison leaned forward. "Lucille, do you think Pete fixed my car?"

"He can tell you himself. He's coming round the dance floor right now." She scooted her chair closer to Allison. "I know you and me got off on the wrong foot, honey. I just want you to know I never meant no harm. Dell's a good man and I wouldn't have minded hooking up with him, but he was never interested."

"And Pete is?" The women shared a smile.

"Oh, he sure is. I thought he was too young for me, but I've decided I like his...energy. Come by the diner sometime and I'll buy you a cup of coffee."

"Thanks. I'd like that."

"Here, honey," Pete said, setting a drink in front of Lucille. He hooked a chair rung with his foot and moved it into place beside his date. "Hey, there, everybody. Dell. Jack. Allison." He nodded at each one in turn. "How y'all doing tonight?"

Allison said hello, but didn't ask about her car. She decided she didn't want to know if the Probe was ready. She wanted to pretend that she was part of Dell's life for just a while longer. She couldn't stay unless he asked her to stay and there was no way to tell if the man was serious or not. But she knew that men didn't want to raise babies—sometimes not even when they were their own—and she didn't expect Dell to want them, either. It was a hard lesson, but she'd learned it well.

The band finished the song and announced that they were taking a break, so the noise level subsided enough that no one had to holler across the table.

"Tell Allison about her car," Lucille said, nudging Pete with her elbow.

Pete glanced at Dell and gulped. He turned to Lucille and put his arm around the back of her chair. "Not much to tell, honey. Besides, I don't feel much like talking business at a dance."

"Since when? You just told Jim McGregor you'd have to order him some new shocks for that old truck."

"That's okay," Allison said quickly. "We don't have to talk about it right now." She scooted her chair over to make room for Kelly, who returned to the table and greeted everyone.

Dell cleared his throat. "So you got that axle rebuilt?"

"Yeah. Came in yesterday. Everything should be set by Monday afternoon."

"Thank you," Allison said, wishing she meant it. She didn't dare ask how much the repair was going to cost and besides, she didn't want to know. She didn't care if she never saw the car again. She wanted to go back to the home that wasn't her home and feed the babies who weren't her babies, crawl into the bed that wasn't her bed next to the man who wasn't really her man at all.

Allison took a sip of her wine and felt completely, one hundred percent pathetic.

NO ONE HAD LAUGHED. At least not to his face. A couple of ranchers from north of town told him they were glad to see him finally getting out. One of their wives said that Allison looked like a nice young woman and wasn't it wonderful of her to take in her sister's children like that.

Obviously, word traveled fast.

He glanced over at Allison as he drove the miles back to the ranch. She had her head back against the seat and he couldn't tell if her eyes were closed or not.

The radio played an old Vince Gill ballad, one of those sad songs about lost love. Hell, he'd be singing those tunes himself in a few days.

Allison would bundle up those girls and leave. Unless he did something to stop her, of course. And then she'd politely turn him down and they'd both be embarrassed. A woman like Allison didn't belong on the Lazy J.

"Dell?" Her voice was soft in the darkness.

"I thought you were asleep."

"No. Just thinking."

He waited for her to continue since she sounded like she had something on her mind, but she didn't say anything. "Thinking about what?" he asked after another mile passed.

"About the car being ready."

She would be anxious to get going. She would want to be on her way to Seattle and her fancy life. "I'll pick it up for you on Monday."

There was a silence. "Thank you," she said, and that was all she said until they pulled up in front of the house. They walked in quietly, through the back door, to find Calvin sprawled on the couch and snoring like an old bear. Allison went right to the babies' room and came back to whisper that they were still asleep. Dell saw from the kitchen clock that it was after midnight already.

"I guess I'd better leave Cal on the couch," Dell said.

"I hope the girls didn't wear him out too much."

"Don't worry about it," he said, following her to the hall. "He's like a mother hen with her chicks. I never would have guessed."

"Me, either." She paused before walking down the

hall. "That was a really nice evening." Allison hesitated in the hall. "I guess I'd better get to bed."

"Yeah. Me, too." He stood looking at her and trying to memorize the way she looked in the dim light. She was all shadows and golden hair. He couldn't tell if she smiled when she good-night, but he stepped toward her anyway. She came into his arms and he bent his head to touch his lips to hers. He didn't intend to kiss her with anything but a casual good-night, but he couldn't help but kiss her with all the passion and longing that was in his heart, as if he could tell her that he loved her with only one kiss in only one moment.

It would have to be enough, he thought, releasing her. There was no question of making love to her tonight, not with Calvin on the couch and no telling when the children would wake and need their mother. It was better that it ended now, before he got in so deep he couldn't get out. Before he drowned from the pain of losing her.

Unless, he thought, going into his empty bedroom and shutting the door behind him. Unless there was a way to convince her to stay. A way that would give them all what they needed.

12

"WHAT'S GOIN' ON, Cal?" Cussy, his horse trailing behind him, stopped the older man as he came out of the main barn. "Heard the boss has gone to town to get the little gal's car."

"Yep." Cal sighed. "He took Rob with him to drive the truck back."

"We've all got money ridin' on this one." Cussy shook his head. "Dell didn't look too good this mornin'. He didn't say two damn words to anyone, 'cept to tell Rob to meet him out front after lunch."

"We might as well get used to it. When Miz Allison and those babies leave the ranch, Dell could turn mean."

"Rob's gonna be out fifty bucks. And you and I are gonna be the big winners," Cussy drawled, but he didn't look any happier about it than Calvin felt. "From the looks of things, looks like we'll be the only ones... Shoot, Cal. That little gal shouldn't leave. Can't you do anything to stop it?"

Lord knows he would if he could. "Dell's the only one who can ask her to stay, and don't you think that boy has too much pride. He's sure she'd turn him down. You know how he is."

Cussy sighed. They all knew how Dell was. Stubborn. And no lady-killer, that's for sure. "The poor boy never could figure out how to sweet-talk a woman."

"Nobody's talkin' to anyone else this mornin'. It's a damn morgue in there." Sure, the babies smiled at him, but they didn't know what was going on. Allison had thanked him for the enchilada recipe as if he'd given her a sackful of gold. He'd been glad to see the dish come back empty. He'd be glad to teach her how to make cinnamon rolls, too.

If she'd stay.

Cussy swung himself onto his horse. "I gotta get back or the boys will figure I've gone to Cheyenne. When's she leaving?"

"In the morning. First thing, she says."

"Damn. Well, it was fun while it lasted."

"Yep. Sure was." Cal watched Cussy ride off, then he shook his head and walked back to the house to see if Allison needed any help with the girlies. It was a sorry deal when a man could win fifty dollars and feel sorrowful about it. Calvin pulled his handkerchief from his back pocket and wiped his nose.

He must be getting old.

THE PROBE returned at two-thirty, but Dell didn't. He'd taken the truck and gone on to Cheyenne, Rob explained. He gave Allison the repair bill to pay on her way out of town tomorrow, tipped his hat and hurried outside. Allison figured the sight of a teary-eyed woman scared him half out of his wits.

SHE'D SPENT the afternoon watching the girls play on her bed. She wanted to keep them out of their car seats today; they'd be in them long enough this week. So she watched them kick their chubby legs and wave their hands in the air trying to catch hold of the matching pink rattles she'd bought in Kansas City and she'd blinked back tears and told herself she must be coming down with a cold.

It wasn't one of her better days.

"I put one of them frozen chicken pot pies in the oven for you," Calvin said at suppertime. "Takes about an hour to cook through." He picked up his hat and jammed it on his head. "Don't let it burn."

"I won't." She knew better than to ask him if he wanted to stay and share the meal with her. He liked the social life of the bunkhouse in the evening, unless there was something special that he wanted to watch on Dell's big-screen television.

"Dell will most likely be home pretty soon." Cal glanced at the clock and shoved his hands into his jeans' pockets. "It's not like him to be gone this long without tellin' anyone where he's goin'."

"He probably had business to do." That's what she'd been telling herself all day. Dell wouldn't be avoiding her, avoiding any potentially embarrassing conversations about the future, would he? He needn't have taken the trouble. She certainly wasn't going to bring up the fact that she'd fallen in love with him.

Who'd believe it? Mayme sure wouldn't. Or maybe she would, but Allison wasn't calling her again until she reached her destination. She'd left a message on Mayme's machine telling her not to encourage Ryan to drive to Seattle next week. Two months ago she'd been engaged to marry someone else, she'd helped run a successful business and she'd thought she had her life all planned. Then Sandy died, the babies came and Ryan bowed out. And now she'd fallen in love with a rancher who'd picked her up on the side of a muddy road and brought her home.

It wasn't as if he was in love with her. Oh, he'd appreciate any woman who smiled at him and treated him nice. Living the way he did, the man was a walking target.

Allison walked through the living room and on to the front porch. It had been cleaned up and Dell had had one of the men slap on a fresh coat of white paint. She shouldn't leave before selecting the furniture and finishing the project, but it was better for everyone if she left. The box marked Marianna's Toys sat, still unopened, by the door. That old shed probably contained a lot of treasures that everyone had forgotten. Allison looked toward the road, hoping to see Dell's truck heading her way. She didn't get her wish, though she waited on the porch for a long time.

Allison shivered and, taking a deep breath so she wouldn't cry, turned around and went to her room. He wasn't coming, and that was that. Besides, she had to finish packing. It was time to move on with her life.

EVERYTHING HAD GONE wrong. Everything had taken too much time. Dell drove up late to find the house dark. They would all be sleeping, getting ready for a big day of traveling tomorrow. Hell. Hell and damnation. He cursed salespeople who figured he had lots of time to kill and lines at the bank and a truck that blew a rear tire thirty miles from home.

He parked the truck next to Allison's Probe and gave the little car a fierce look. The little son of a bitch better take good care of Allison and those kids. Dell went inside through the back door and listened hard to hear if Allison was awake and feeding the babies. Nope, he'd missed her.

But she was still here. He patted his front pocket to make sure it was still there, and smiled when he felt the little circle. Yep, she was still on the Lazy J. There was still a chance to keep her here.

"ANYONE SEEN HIM?" Allison asked Cal. She poured herself a cup of coffee and looked outside at the dawn. The girls had been awake since five and were impatiently waiting to be fed.

"Nope." Sophie let out a shriek and Calvin hurried to adjust his hearing aid. "Though I sure as hell would like to have a little talk with him myself."

"Do you think he'll say goodbye?"

The old man shrugged. "I dunno. I finally figured out that I don't know anything."

"Me, too," Allison sighed. "All I know is that I've got two kids to take care of and a job waiting for me in Seattle. It's a good job, too. With benefits."

Cal nodded. "Sounds nice. I heard it rains a lot there, though. The girlies aren't going to go outside and play."

"It's not *that* rainy," she assured him. "It's a beautiful city. I went to college there."

The old man didn't look impressed. He picked up Sophie and told her to be quiet. Allison handed him a bottle and then turned to Sylvie, who opened her mouth to scream. "Stop that. You don't want to wake up Dell."

"I'll wake him up," Cal muttered, frowning. "I'd sure as hell like to know where he was yesterday."

"He must have had business in the city." *He must have been avoiding me.*

"Business." Cal shook his head. "He had business *here.*"

Allison found a paper napkin and wiped her eyes.

"I'm sure it was something important, Cal. It takes a lot for Dell to leave this ranch."

"Humph," was all the old man had to say. Allison carried Sylvie into the living room and sat in the rocking chair to feed her. She admired the way the large cupboard gleamed from the three polishings she'd given it. Even the battered coffee table looked better with a layer of polish and a good scrubbing. She'd debated about whether or not to keep it, but it was the kind of table that was accustomed to boot heels and beer bottles, wet glasses and warm plates. It belonged here.

She didn't.

HE COULD HEAR them out in the kitchen. Cal was grumbling and making more noise in the sink than was necessary. Dell almost smiled. The old man was most likely trying to wake him up without banging on the door and making it obvious. His uncle would be happy thinking he was going to have the kitchen to himself again.

Well, he could think again. Dell looked at the alarm clock by his bed. Still early. He had time to clean up and make a good impression. He took a long shower and put on a clean shirt. He made sure his hair was combed, and he waited for the nick on his chin to stop bleeding.

Thirty minutes later he stood in the kitchen doorway and said good morning. "Where are the girls?"

"They've gone back to bed," Allison said, taking a sip of her coffee before arranging empty bottles on the counter. She was already dressed and her hair was pulled back in a low ponytail. He wondered how long she'd been up. He wondered if she was packed, but then realized she would need help carrying all that stuff to the car. And if the babies were asleep, Allison couldn't put their playpen in the Probe. He still had some time.

"You're still leaving this morning?"

"Yes."

"When?"

"After the girls wake up. After I pack the car."

"I took it for a test run. Pete did a good job."

She opened a can of formula and didn't look at him. "Rob gave me the bill. I'll stop in Wells City and pay it on my way out."

"It's out of your way."

Allison shrugged. "That's all right."

Calvin muttered something under his breath, grabbed his hat and stomped out the back door.

"What's the matter with him?" Dell asked.

Allison opened another can. "I don't know. He's a little edgy this morning, I guess."

Dell poured himself a cup of coffee, but set it on the counter without tasting it. He moved a few steps closer and figured it was now or never. His heart pounded like he'd just lifted one end of a horse. He wondered if he was having a heart attack or if this was just part of dealing with women. He took a deep breath.

"Are you okay?" Allison asked. "You look a little pale."

"I could use a wife around here," Dell announced. Allison was at the counter fixing baby bottles. Some of the milk spilled and she grabbed a sponge and started wiping it up.

"I'm sure you could," she replied, not looking at him. "It's not healthy to live in such an isolated place and be alone all the time." She snapped the plastic nipples and caps on the bottles and took them over to the refrigerator.

Dell figured he hadn't phrased that right.

"I meant you," he said, standing there as helpless as a newborn calf in a ditch. "You need a husband and I need a wife. It could work. Marriage, I mean."

Allison shut the refrigerator door and turned to face him. "What are you saying, Dell?"

He stood his ground. "I'm asking you to marry me."

Those blue eyes blinked. "Because you need a wife?"

He nodded. Thank goodness she understood. "Yep."

"And you think I need a husband."

"You do," he agreed. "You need someone to take care of you and those babies."

She looked at him as if she was waiting for him to say something else.

"You need *me*," he explained. "And you know it."

"I see."

"It could work." He didn't tell her how much he loved her. He didn't want to scare her off. "It's worked so far, hasn't it?"

Allison didn't answer his question, but instead asked one of her own. "Why do you want me to marry you, Dell?"

*Because I love you so much that the thought of losing you makes me want to throw myself in front of a herd of stampeding horses.* "A lot of reasons. Those girls need a father. You need a husband. I hate to see you taking off all by yourself. It's a long way to Seattle."

"I'll be all right. I have a job waiting for me when I get there." Her voice was quiet.

"You and the girls could have a good home here," he

countered. "You'd never have to worry about anything, 'cept maybe the weather. I wouldn't mind having a son or two, but it's okay, too, if it's just the girls."

She didn't say anything, but her face had gone pale.

Dell took a swallow of hot coffee and hoped he hadn't scared her. "Think it over."

"I don't have to." He noticed her hands shook as she reached for the sponge and wiped the already clean counter. "I can't stay," she said. "Not like that."

His heart grew cold in his chest. "Well, hell, I guess I should've known better than to bring it up."

"You just feel sorry for me," she said.

Dell found he couldn't speak. He'd counted on her staying. He'd counted on her seeing the practical reasons why it would be for the best. He hadn't thought she'd say no just like that.

He walked by her and took his hat off the peg. It took every ounce of self-control he had not to gather her in his arms and carry her off to bed. He wanted to make love to her until she agreed to stay. Until she smiled and kissed him and told him to put the Probe in one of the sheds because she wouldn't be needing it right away.

Instead Dell kept walking, through the storeroom and out the back door. He'd made her a fair proposal. He'd done all he could do. Saying anything about love would just be making himself look like a fool.

ALLISON STOOD at the counter and watched out the window as Dell hunched his shoulders against the wind and strode toward the large bunkhouse. He'd left her alone in the kitchen. He hadn't told her he loved her or taken her in his arms. She gave him credit for not being a hypocrite.

She watched until he disappeared from her sight, until the tears that she refused to shed blurred her vision. He didn't love her. Oh, he needed her. Just like Ryan needed her to help run the business. Well, she'd told him no and she told Dell the same thing. Wendell Jones needed a wife. Any woman would do. He hadn't come down from his ranch to go search for one, but having a woman come right into the ranch made the job easy.

Damn the man.

She loved him. And if she married him she'd love him even more. She'd fix up the ranch and the bunkhouses and she'd have a few more children and she'd learn how to ride a horse faster than a trot. She'd be happy to stop decorating other people's houses and concentrate on her own. She wanted to bake cupcakes for birthday parties and talk about babies with the other young mothers in town. She wanted to be in love with her husband, and she wanted to be loved by him so much that when he smiled at her she'd know she was the most important person in his life.

She couldn't settle for anything less. Allison turned from the window and wiped her eyes on a paper napkin. It was time to leave.

SHE WAS LEAVING, but he'd be damned if he was going to make it easy for her. Cussy and Jed were still around, so they were given the job of carrying Allison's belongings to the car. Calvin banged pots and pans in the kitchen and gave Dell dirty looks whenever he got the chance. Like it was his fault Allison and the girlies were leaving.

Allison's eyes were rimmed with red, but she talked with Calvin about the days of traveling ahead. Dell hung back, afraid to open his mouth and say the wrong thing. And yet, things couldn't get much worse.

Until Allison hesitated on the front porch and pointed to the unopened box that had belonged to his grandmother. "Don't you want to know what's inside?"

"It doesn't matter," he said, folding his arms across his chest. He had no use for toys, and never would. Allison turned away and hurried outside for yet another trip to check the car while Dell stood on the porch and felt completely helpless. He wanted to put his fist through the freshly painted wall. On the next trip, she carried the babies, and this time Dell's heart rose to his throat and threatened to choke him. He didn't dare touch them or say a word.

When the Probe was loaded, the babies fastened in their car seats and the cooler filled with the baby bottles, he thought saying goodbye to the girls would kill him, but he managed to stay upright as the pain radiated through his body.

"Thank you," she said. "For everything." She gave him a quick hug, but moved away before he could make his frozen arms wrap around her. Allison kissed Cal on the cheek.

"I've got copies of all your best recipes," she said. "Thanks for sharing."

"Just do 'em justice," he growled. "Though you might want to go easy on the hot sauce when the girlies are old enough to eat my food."

"I will," she promised. She turned to Jed and Cussy, who removed their hats and accepted her thanks for all of their help. Then, with car keys in hand, she stepped toward Dell, raised up on her toes and kissed him briefly on the lips. He got a quick glimpse of tears before she slid behind the steering wheel and shut the door. The engine roared to life, the men stepped out of the way so she could back the car up and head down the drive.

Cussy and Cal took out handkerchiefs and blew their noses loudly. Jed gulped as he glanced at Dell and turned away.

"Doesn't anyone have work to do around here?" Dell roared.

"Hell, yes," Cussy said, backing up. He grabbed the younger man's arm and hurried him out of the line of fire. Dell stomped back into the house, with his uncle close behind.

He hesitated on the porch and turned to watch the cloud of dust behind the Probe. She was driving slowly, but the car was heading in a direct line to the main road.

"What're you bawling for? I thought you didn't want a woman around here."

Cal sniffed. "I could've been a grandpa. I could've been, too, if you had asked that woman to stay."

"I asked her to stay," Dell muttered.

"Well, you musta messed it up then," the old cowboy grumped. He wiped his eyes and kicked the unopened box out of his way. "Open this goddamn thing or let me put it back in the shed."

"Got no use for toys," Dell snapped. He watched the little car continue slowly on its way out of his life as Cal took out his pocketknife and slit through the tape holding the box together. "Never will."

Cal unwrapped a wad of newspaper. "Why, it's two little wooden animals. Sheep, I think." He reached in and continued to unwrap sets of animals, and lined them up two-by-two under the window. He pulled out a large wooden boat and showed it to Dell. "I think it's s'posed to be Noah's ark. The girlies would love it, when they get a little older."

Dell barely glanced at the wooden figures. The car had slowed down. It may even have stopped, but he couldn't tell. "Put the damn things away," he said. "Where the hell are the binoculars?"

"Hangin' on that nail over there," Cal said. "Two by two," he muttered, struggling to his feet. "Just the way it should be. Not right for a woman to go off alone into the world when there's a man who—"

"Cal, shut up and take a look at this." He handed his uncle the binoculars. "What do you see?"

Calvin adjusted the binoculars and squinted. "She's gone off the road."

"That woman can't drive for beans," Dell declared, a smile crossing his face. "She's stuck."

The older man handed him the binoculars. "So what in hell are you going to do about it? Bring down the tractor and pull her out and send her on her way again?"

"She wouldn't stay. I asked."

"Did you sweet-talk her a little?"

Dell hedged. "I offered her a home."

"Did you tell her you loved her?" Cal shouted. "I'll bet a hundred dollars you kept your mouth shut and that pride of yours right safe, didn't you, son?"

"She couldn't love me. Nothing could be that good."

"Why the hell not?"

He picked up the binoculars again. The car wasn't moving. "Why the hell would she?"

"She didn't care about that face of yours. I think she kinda liked it, myself. That little lady thought you walked on water," Cal declared. "Why, those blue eyes would shine when you came inside for supper and she'd watch you out the window when we was cookin'. I may be deaf, but I'm sure as hell not blind. That woman loves you."

Dell fought the surge of hope that took his heart from his throat and settled it back where it belonged. "She never said anything."

"Why should she? She's been hurt bad. Prob'ly has as much foolish pride as you do." Cal sighed and shook his head. "Young fools." He pointed toward the road. "She's about a mile and a half away. What're you gonna do?"

He readjusted his hat and pushed the door open. "Why, hell, Calvin. I'm going to find out what the lady wants."

ALLISON KNEW she should get out of the car to see what had happened. One minute she'd been speeding down the gravel road and the next thing she knew she'd wished she'd been going slower. The car had shimmied and slid on the dirt, then pitched into a low ditch. She didn't want to get out and see what she had done. Not yet. Not until she'd found a tissue and wiped her nose.

Not until she stopped crying.

The babies had protested at the bumps and now screamed their discontent with life in the back seat of the Probe. Allison didn't try to calm them with soothing words. She felt like screaming, too. She wanted to kick her feet and kick the car, too, while she was kicking things. She wanted to get out of Wyoming and she couldn't even get off the ranch.

She rested her arms against the steering wheel, put

her head down and sobbed until she could hardly
breathe.

"Hell, Allison," a familiar voice drawled. "You don't
drive any better than you ride a horse."

She didn't lift her head. She was a mess and he
didn't have to see it. "I do okay on pavement." She
heard him open her car door. He bent over so close that
she could smell his shaving lotion. The girls stopped
crying when they heard his voice, but the pounding
pain in Allison's temples continued. She hated good-
byes and she hated dirt roads.

"I thought you might have changed your mind
about leaving," he said.

Changed her mind? She wanted to run back to the
house and into the safety of his arms. "No."

"I thought you might have decided you need a husband after all."

"Go away, Dell."

He cleared his throat. "Truth is, Allison, I've never
asked anyone to marry me before. I guess I messed it
up pretty bad. I've never been in love before, either."
She heard him take a deep breath and his boots
crunched in the dust as he crouched to be at the same
level. "Cal says I've got too much pride, and I guess
he's right. So if you don't love me, just tell me. I'll get
the tractor and pull you out of here and you can be on
your way to wherever it is you want to go. But you
should know that I'll love you till the day I die and I'll
do my best to make you and those babies happy if you
marry me."

Allison lifted her head and turned to look at him.
Had he really said he loved her? "Why would you
marry me even if I didn't love you?"

He gulped. "No, I guess I wouldn't want that, after

all. I'd sure as hell want someone who loved me, but I'm willing to bet that you'd come to love me, in time."

"Yes," she said, wiping her eyes. "That would be easy enough. You're a good man, but you should marry someone who knows how to ride and cook and take care of animals."

He frowned. "Why? I have the men for those things."

Allison couldn't help smiling. "Yes, I guess you do."

"Tell me you love me," he said. "One way or the other and we'll go from there."

"Truth is," she said, touching his face with her hand, "I do love you, Wendell Jones. I'm not sure how it happened, but I know I don't want to leave."

"Then get the hell out of that car and come home," Dell said, but Allison didn't move except to put her arms around his neck and kiss him for long, wonderful moments.

"All right," she agreed, stepping out of the car. She resisted the urge to dance with joy. "Which baby do you want?"

"Makes no difference," the cowboy said. "I'll take them both, if you want."

"I guess you're taking all three of us." She paused. "Are you sure, Dell?"

He nodded. "I've got a diamond ring in my dresser drawer. A man doesn't go into a jewelry store in Cheyenne unless he's sure."

"Is that where you were yesterday?"

"Yeah." He waited for her to unbuckle the children from their seats and took Sylvie from Allison's arms. "But I made a mistake."

Allison paused, giving him a worried look. "What do you mean?"

He waved at the car tilted into the ditch. "I should've bought you a truck instead."

She laughed. "First thing, you're going to have to give me driving lessons."

"No, ma'am," Dell said, kissing her once again. "That's not the first thing we're going to do at all."

# ____Epilogue____

THE COWBOYS GATHERED around the table and waited for Calvin to count the money. He took his time, which only made them more anxious, and separated bills into small piles.

"There," he declared, pushing the piles of money toward the winners. "You all were right after all. They're getting married, all right. Soon as possible, Dell said. They've been kissing and hugging and mooning around for three days. Dell got a license in town yesterday and Allison's renting the community center for a big shindig."

"I like being right," Jed said, tucking his winnings into his shirt pocket. "And we need a missus around here. The boss is gonna be real cheerful from now on, don't you think?"

The older men didn't look convinced. Of course, they'd lost a few dollars so they weren't real confident in giving any more romantic opinions.

Rob opened another bottle of beer. "What are you gonna do with all that money you made, Cal? Maybe you've got enough for one of them electric bread machines you've been yapping about for a couple of years."

Cal sat down and leaned back in the chair. "Nope. I've got better ideas."

Cussy sat down beside him. "Don't ask me to bet on what he's buyin', boys. I'm plum broke till payday."

"I figure the missus might get one of them machines for a wedding present." He gave the men a look that told them to pay attention. "Maybe all of you would like to pitch in for that," he suggested, trying not to smile too hard. "Seein' how the lady ain't much of a cook and I might go on vacation once in a while."

Jed nodded and tossed his winnings back into the middle of the table. "Count me in, Cal."

"Me, too," said Jed. The others took money from their pockets and set a stack of bills on the table. "But what are you gonna do with the baby-holding money?"

"Well..." Cal drawled. "Since I'm their new *grandpa*," he said with relish, "I have certain rights."

Cussy glared at him. "Quit actin' so damn mysterious and spit it out."

The old man gave a satisfied sigh and pulled out a worn deck of cards. "I've got my eye on a pair of matching ponies, and if anyone wants to play a little poker tonight, I might just earn enough for a couple of saddles, too."

## Cowboys and babies

Roping, riding and ranching are part of cowboy life.
Diapers, pacifiers and formula are not!

At least, not until three sexy cowboys from three great
states face their greatest challenges and rewards when
confronted with a little bundle of joy.

#617 THE LAST MAN IN MONTANA (January)
#621 THE ONLY MAN IN WYOMING (February)
#625 THE NEXT MAN IN TEXAS (March)

Fan favorite Kristine Rolofson has created a wonderful
miniseries with all the appeal of the great American West
and the men and women who love the land.

Three rugged cowboys, three adorable babies—what
heroine could resist!

Available wherever Harlequin books are sold.

# Take 4 bestselling love stories FREE

## Plus get a FREE surprise gift!

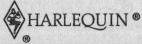

# Heartbreak RANCH

Four generations of independent women...
Four heartwarming, romantic stories of the West...
Four incredible authors...

## Fern Michaels
## Jill Marie Landis
### Dorsey Kelley
### Chelley Kitzmiller

Saddle up with Heartbreak Ranch, an outstanding
Western collection that will take you on a whirlwind
trip through four generations and the exciting,
romantic adventures of four strong women who
have inherited the ranch from Bella Duprey,
famed Barbary Coast madam.

Available in March,
wherever Harlequin books are sold.

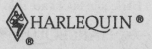

HARLEQUIN ®
®

# LOVE *or* MONEY?
## Why not Love *and* Money!
### After all, millionaires need love, too!

## How to Marry a
# MILLIONAIRE

## Suzanne Forster,
## Muriel Jensen
## and
## Judith Arnold

bring you three original stories
about finding that one-in-a-million man!

Harlequin also brings you
a million-dollar sweepstakes—enter
for your chance to win a fortune!

*You are cordially invited to a*

# HOMETOWN REUNION

### *September 1996—August 1997*

Bad boys, cowboys, babies. Feuding families,
arson, mistaken identity, a mom on the run…
Where can you find romance and adventure?
Tyler, Wisconsin, that's where!

So join us in this not-so-sleepy little town and
experience the love, the laughter and the
tears of those who call it home.

## WELCOME TO A
# HOMETOWN REUNION

Gabe Atwood has no sooner rescued his wife,
Raine, from a burning building when there's
more talk of fires. Rumor has it that Clint
Stanford suspects Jon Weiss, the new kid at
school, of burning down the Ingallses' factory.
And that Marina, Jon's mother, has kindled a fire
in Clint that may be affecting his judgment. Don't
miss Kristine Rolofson's *A Touch of Texas,*
the seventh in a series you won't want to end….

Available in March 1997
at your favorite retail store.

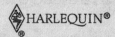

HARLEQUIN®

Look us up on-line at: http://www.romance.net          HTR7

# *You're About to Become a*
# *Privileged*
# *Woman*

Reap the rewards of fabulous free gifts and
benefits with proofs-of-purchase from
Harlequin and Silhouette books

# Pages & Privileges™

It's our way of thanking you for
buying our books at your
favorite retail stores.

PROOF OF
PURCHASE  HT-PP22
Offer expires March 31,1997

Harlequin and Silhouette—
the most privileged readers in the world!

For more information about Harlequin and
Silhouette's PAGES & PRIVILEGES program call the
Pages & Privileges Benefits Desk: 1-503-794-2499

HARLEQUIN ®

HT-PP22